COPING WITH THE TEALERS

JAMES E. D. CLINE

DEDICATION

This book is dedicated to the memory of Hulda R. Clark, PhD, in appreciation for her altruistic writings giving away her inventions in electroherbalism bioresonance and the basic "zapper" that shows a way for economical future health of people around the world, particularly in emergency situations requiring self-help.

CONTENTS

ACKNOWLEDGMENTS

Hulda Clark's writings inspired some of the key chapters of this book involving healing in dire circumstances. And in a very different field of endeavor, appreciation is also given to the American Society of Civil Engineers, who saw the KESTS to GEO transportation concept as a civil engineering project, thus bypassing the decade of aerospace suppression of the author's many concepts related to the KESTS to GEO, Space Carousel Escalator internally-generated centrifugal force supported transportation structure ground to space, and the many kinds of facilities it would make feasible in GEO such as the orbiting solar powered total recycler facilities. An extension of the concept is also key to this story.

Jim Cline
Ephrata, WA, USA December 14, 2013
Revised January 10, 2014

1 HERMIT'S SURVIVAL

This way of life would be called a hermit, he groused. Not my choice, he said to himself; but despite all his efforts there was no woman being his companion and mate. So, hermit it is. Maybe in the future, things would change, was his hope. But for now, he had to survive, and learn what he could about the situation.

The air, the ground, everything was getting cold. the long winter was going to happen and he was out here. At least he was alive. When the bunch of Tealer men had turned on him and attacked in town, apparently because he had tried to be friendly to one of the womenfolk there, he had been a bit slow in figuring out that those men considered all the town's women were theirs, despite their mistreatment of the women. He still could not remember much else, other than he slowly was recovering from a gash wound healing up, and he still was in a daze from some kind of head wound. Fortunately there was plenty of food on the trees and bushes out here, and the small springs provided refreshing drink and for splashing on his face, sometimes washing away old caked blood. Something had happened - oh yes, there was that bunch of men who had suddenly attacked him near his house. But where town was, how to get back to his home, was too much of a puzzle right now. Even the terrain here was not quite like anything he had seen from the edge of town where he had lived.

He had found a trail of damage to the small herbal grasses, leading down the side of the cliff, which apparently was made as he dropped down the face of the cliff. Some of it was going together in his mind, but mostly was unknowns, and besides he could not think for very long without the headache coming back and distraction lost the train of thought. He had these clothes he wore but the pockets were empty. The only tool he had was the short length of rope which he had been able to untie from where they had bound his wrists. The piece of rope was now in a pocket, at least something to work with.

He sought to find some place further away from the base of the cliff, the many human remains that littered the area spoke of this being a disposal site for men. That he apparently had snagged on a projecting bush from the face of the cliff, which had broken his fall enough to divert his evident path the rest of the way down, tumbling, leaving the trail of broken vegetation, wrapped up in the bush.

Even if he could figure out how to get back home, right now that did not look like it would increase his survival chances. All his belongings in his house would probably be gone, someone else living there, probably some woman set up in there for the gang of Tealer men to breed.

He was lucky to be alive, unlike the other men who lay below the cliff, in various stages of disintegration. Some were bleached skeletons; others were probably only weeks there. It was not a place he wanted to be. Yet after a few days he had gone back to see if any of the remains had anything useful as a tool, but all clearly had had their pockets emptied, just like his had been. From then on, he just tried to find which way was upwind from there.

Back to his immediate survival situation, he could not bring himself to remove any of the tattered clothing from those other unfortunates at the base of the cliff. And his clothes were not adequate to keep away the cold at night, he had already figured out. Things faded away and then he became more conscious again, his head hurt and was swollen, and he felt a bit nauseated. A concussion, that was what it was, he remembered. Really needed to not be very active now. But he was also getting colder, dusk was approaching. Looking around for anything like some shelter, he found one of the fruit trees that had turned gray and had no leaves or fruit; the pile of dried leaves at its base might be insulation in the night.

The mild breeze would still soak away his body heat, he knew. He broke off a branch from the tree, and used it to stir the leaves around; they seemed quite deep. He continued to dig away the leaves, heaping them to be a bit of piled shield upwind of the hole he was digging. One arm hurt too much to help more than guide the stick, while the uninjured arm did the work dragging the stick back and forth in the leaves. Slowly a trench was formed; the lower leaves had been packed with the years, and did not fall back into the trench he was making. A few more smaller branches broken off, placed across part of the trench, then they were covered with leaves, a kind of roof. And as the light faded too much to see to work, he lay down in the trench, his upper torso under the little roofed area, and he pulled leaves down over his lower body in the trench in the leaves.

He lay there, relaxing and noticing the near silence out there. A bit of rustling of the leaves where he had stirred them up, at times. He dragged some leaves over all but his face; and indeed he was already feeling warmer. A wave of dizziness and nausea filled his consciousness for awhile, then faded. At least he was warm and resting.

He awoke to a beam of sunlight coming down in a gap in the roof over his head. He was not hurting so much now. He was also feeling thirsty and hungry. He remembered the abundant edibles of the area, and the small springs that would refresh him. Digging himself out from under the leaves in the trench, he got a look at how well the leaves had packed under the old tree. This might be a place to set up a longer term shelter; he had not found any natural shelter anywhere in the past couple of days wandering here. For now, he would simply circle the spot, gathering some fruit and other edibles, find a spring, and go from there. That was about all the planning he could do for now; his head hurt and he kept forgetting what he had been thinking about.

After he had circled a bit, picking berries while eating some and putting others in his pocket, he realized he had lost sight of his new home. He retraced the trail he had made to get here, and eventually found the little leaf trench again; he decided to only walk straight away from the place, then reverse direction and walk straight back here. That worked fairly well; and he also had oriented to the huge wall of the cliff, its shapes, and that helped him orient to his warm nighttime abode. The resulting tracks through the low brush and ground cover, soon all pointed to one place; he hoped there were no predators that might follow them. But he had seen no indication of anything big enough to make a trail through the plants here, other than himself. If any other men who had been tossed off the cliff had survived, they were not around here anymore. He had looked up the cliff from the place where he had landed among the other human remains, and it was a high cliff indeed. Going back there now, he found an uprooted bush, roots and all, apparently was what had broken his fall partway up the cliff; its bare roots somehow reminded him of himself, so he picked it up and carried it back to his new shelter area, dug a hole in the nearest dirt area that was sunny, and replanted the bush there, maybe it would take root and live. Almost a symbol of himself, he mused. And it needed water too; some to help survive until the drizzly rain was enough to rebuild its fine root structure.

Recalling a gourd plant he had encountered in one of his linear forays from his little shelter, and finding it again, he gathered a couple gourds from the ground that were dried and hard; perhaps he could convert them into water carriers and even storage for water. How to open the gourds and shape the opening for his application, would be something he would have to work on later; he had no cutting tool yet.

His next linear foray from his trench home, as it was getting to be dusk again, went direct to the nearest face of the cliff wall. He thought that he could find home again by walking straight out from that wall of rock. Picking up some rock shards that looked like they could be used for cutting things, he turned and walked straight away from the rock face, counting the number of steps he had taken to get there. It was enough even in the dim light to find his little burrow, and soon he was back inside, now with a couple of gourds and several sharp rock pieces. Covering his torso with leaves again, soon he was asleep, his head under the little roof he had made.

Awakening to small streams of sunlight through the makeshift covering over his head the next morning, his thoughts were a little clearer this time. He remembered he had gourds for storage use, and sharp rocks for cutting the gourds. That there were the remains of many less fortunate men lying not that far away, also was in remembrance as he began to stir. Tossing the leaves off his lower torso, he sat up in his makeshift shelter. Finding pocketfuls of berries, he began savoring them, starting his morning.

As a hermit. There was no woman available for him as partner, lover, mate, companion in accomplishing things of life. None. Not that the women had no one for me so much as that the gang of men had found they could reproduce with all the women, by eliminating all the other men. Like all those remains not so far way but fortunately downwind. Almost also himself. Yet also himself, in effect. The women of the town had no choice, breed with the gang of Tealer men, or leave no progeny.

The handy berries were flavorful and provided liquid and nourishment. The dizzy moments, the nausea, the forgetting what he had been intending to do, was less now.

He cleared out his little trench of the leaves that had kept him warm overnight. He picked up one of the sharper looking rocks, and began to tap away with it along an imaginary circle on one of the gourds. A few times around, and the gourd came in two; the larger part had seeds and debris that were easily removed. He carefully set most of the seeds aside, yet also scattering a few of them on the ground outside his little abode; maybe they would grow there someday. But for now, he needed to test if the gourd could hold water.

He filled the gourd from the nearest spring, drank some of it, then carried it refilled over to the little bush he had replanted, the bush that had saved his life in his unconscious fall down here. He poured the water around where the roots were in the dirt. Hopefully the drizzly rain would then finish the nourishment of this cherished bush. He resolved to bring more water over here at other times, too.

Then he went back to the spring, refilled the gourd, took it back to his little trench abode, setting it inside upright. Later he would see if it indeed kept the water inside. Then he used the sharp edge of the broken rock to similarly open up the other gourd, and soon it was ready for use in storage, and its seeds had been saved too, as well as a few seeds tossed off to the side of his abode, might grow there sometime. But for now, he was beginning to realize he needed a larger abode than this little trench.

Where to make his hermit home, he pondered. Just below the face of the rock wall cliff would be a place to build a sturdier shelter, perhaps. But right now he liked this place, snuggled beneath the remains of an old tree, warmed by its layers of old leaves it had produced and dropped over unknown numbers of winters.

He could break off more branches from the old tree. He could use the sharp rock to cut through even larger dried up branches, to make longer spans for supporting roof material. Yet he was seeing himself like this old tree; dead that the tree was, it had provides quick shelter for him. Maybe he could just make a larger abode off to the side of the old leafless tree. The deep layers of old leaves seemed excellent insulation for the cold.

Although he did not recognize this ecosystem, it apparently was far from his home, and its cold nights suggested that it might become a long very cold wintry place to live. The packed leaves might provide significant preservation of his body heat, maybe the only source of heat in the too near future. Climbing the walls of the cliff seemed out of his ability for now; and what was above was unknown, surely at least at times would be the gang of guys bringing another potentially reproductive rival man to toss off the cliff. Not the kind of folks he would expect to help him.

The second gourd made a fine holder for the nuts and berries he gathered the next day. The berries would not last long; but the nuts could provide him some nourishment even if trapped in some shelter he built here. He went to gather more of the dried gourds; storage containers for the winter were looking increasingly important right now. He was careful to plant a few of the seeds of each plant from which he gathered seeds and nuts for the winter. He planted them both near the mother tree and also scattered further away, in possibly sunny areas. He would help the plants flourish, even as they helped him survive, at least for now.

He found an even older broken up tree, and gathered its branches to be brought over to build a larger roofed trench in his new home. How cold would it get here this winter? He decided to dig the tunnel much deeper in the leaf layers, and then used the new large branches to provide a support framework for smaller branches, then to support clumps of leaves brought up from his diggings below. He decided to make the depth of the leaf layer above to be equal to the length of his forearm. And the span of the roof was made the same as his height, so he could be completely under it if need be. He hollowed out some side areas, and began to stash gourds filled with berries, seeds and nuts.

Yet the increasingly cold nights showed that even covering his torso and legs with leaves, was not enough to stay warm. and he suspected that winter's world was going to be a lot tougher than now. Man had always used fire for warmth when it got too cold for his own body heat to maintain a survival shelter. Building a fire in this highly flammable leaf and branch shelter seemed risky, even if he had a way to start a fire.

For now he could concentrate on insulation to conserve body heat. Yet he had to be able to breathe, and the air would be very cold. How much body heat would the stored dried fruit seeds and nuts would provide him, was unknown.

He lost count of the days and nights since awakening down here, but it seemed like a dozen days had passed by the time he had built a fully roofed-over abode under the leaves, and had used some gourds cut at both ends to make a ventilation pipe above a small hearth made of rocks he had brought from near the cliff wall. If he could get a small fire started, he ought to be able to keep it going there, and bring in fresh air for the fire and for him to breathe. He looked for stones that might be struck together to make a spark, but no flint was found, nor did any of these rocks make a spark when struck together. He vaguely remembered there was a way to use a thong to twirl a stick to heat an area with friction enough to start a small fire, which then could be fed to be a sufficiently large fire.

Fire would also provide some light in the darkness. It was a worthy goal, he told himself. Yet living in a flammable abode that provides wonderful insulation, seemed unwise. He brought over more stones from the rock wall face, and built a containment bowl for the hypothetical fire.

2   COMPANION ARRIVES THE HARD WAY

He remembered that primitive man had advanced by making tools that amplified his own abilities, then from them to make more tools that enabled him to do even other kinds of things. The making of tools, therefore, seemed a worthy goal, even making tools that did not seem needed immediately. He was having more time that was optional as to what he did in the time; yet also the wintertime was setting in too.

He had a nicely insulated home under the branches of the old tree, a door that seemed to seal shut fairly well, rows of gourds filled with seeds and nuts and dried fruit, even some roots he had found edible. Other gourds had water in them, yet how long the water would remain healthy, was unknown.

What would happen to the springs when winter came in full force? Would they freeze up or lose their water source? Could he rely on being able to get to the springs for water in the harsh winter?

The direction of the wind became more variable too, as cold weather advanced. He had built a fairly solid hoe from a branch and a suitable shard of rock, although he would have preferred a better binding of the two than the still green vines of the area. He dug graves for some of the men, starting with the newer ones, less for respect for them than for reducing the odors that sometimes went to his abode.

He was out there digging another grave for the past men tossed off the cliff, when he noticed a noise from far above him, high on the edge of the cliff wall. He quickly moved to hide under a tree, lest they spot him and resume efforts to dispose of him. He tried to see what was going on up there, but it seemed like a fight was going on. Had he put up a fight before being tossed down here? He could not remember. It seemed his hands had been bound and probably he was brought unconscious and tossed over the cliff. But, he was not sure. He had hit his head hard, on the fall down here, and probably was clubbed even before that.

He only could hear bits of voices far up there, not comprehensible, but some of the voices seemed different than the others. then a body smacked down on the ground not far away; it lay motionless, another luckless man, way too mangled to survive; the man moved around a bit, then lay motionless. Yet more noises, voices seemed angry from far above on top of the cliff.

Suddenly several bodies landed in a heap all at once. What was going on up there? It was silence up there now, however. Apparently the clump of people of the latest batch had solved the problem of the noisemakers far above. He was only a little curious about the new arrivals; they would be more to bury. Maybe he ought to get with it right away. The ground had begun to get frozen hard on the surface by morning, and would be harder to dig graves the longer he waited.

But a whole clump of people? There had been no indication that more than one had fallen down here at a time before. Going over to the newcomers, he noticed one of them looked familiar, maybe even one of the men who he vaguely remembered had assaulted him. That did not make sense. He pulled the clump of people apart, ready to bury them, five people. Then he noticed that two of them were not men; they were women. Apparently some women had spotted the gang of men and had followed them to where they were disposing of non-member men. Maybe some of the women had objected to that and had begun a fight up there, and thus the man who had been one of those who had tossed him down here, was now dead down here too.

A lot of new people to bury, five of them. Whatever was going on up above, seemed to be over; no more bodies were falling down.

Burying the women was the hardest part. Dragging the second woman over to a small trench he had dug with his makeshift hoe, it seemed she had moved a bit of her own; she had been on top of the pile, cushioned by the others. Yes, on inspection, she seemed to be breathing. A broken leg and a broken arm, what else. He would see if she could be kept alive awhile; she seemed too mangled to live long, but he ought to help her insofar as he could. He got some sticks and set the broken arm and leg and tied them to the splints made of tree branches. He was glad she was unconscious; that would have hurt a lot, he thought. Yet, it was getting cold, sun starting to go down.

He made a drag stretcher of two long branches, and tugged her toward his abode. But it had gotten dark, where was his abode? She at least seemed to be wearing winter apparel, that could help her. In fact, he noticed bulges in her pockets; she had not been treated as the men, apparently not intended to be tossed down here. He felt around in her pockets, and found a lighter. In moments he had a small torch lit. He made two of them, putting one in the ground next to where she lay on the stretcher so he could find her, and the other for him to wander around in search of where he was.

It took only moments to find his pathway from the graveyard to his underground home, and soon he was tugging the stretcher along toward his abode, carrying a burning torch. He ought to be able to make her a little more comfortable in there, until he would have to bury her too.

Into the shelter, door closed; he tested his little hearth with the small torch, using the light to cover the woman with leaves for insulation. Then he blew the torch out regretfully, but he could not stay awake all night watching to see it did not get out of control. He collapsed from exhaustion, a few leaves on top of himself and was soon asleep.

The sound of moaning and a bit of sunlight making its way through his roof, awoke him. Moaning, and it was not himself moaning this time. He was still a bit dizzy and forgetful from the concussion, but more things were making a bit of sense. The moaning was another person.

He had brought a badly injured woman down in here last night, yes, that was it. It was cold in here, He remembered the lighter that he had gotten from the woman's pocket, and lit the torch in his hearth. He arranged more leaves and twigs; he hoped to not have to use the lighter again. He went over to the woman still on the stretcher, with the crudely made splints on one arm and opposite leg. She seemed to be still breathing. He put a few drops of water into her mouth, from one of his gourds. Then propping her upper torso up a bit on the stretcher, he gave her more water. It seemed it was being kept in this time not just dribbled out. He took a chance and put one of the more flavorful berries between her lips; she seemed unconscious. Yet a few moments later when he looked back at here, the little fruit was gone, and had not just fallen down. He looked thoughtfully at her.

Something looked familiar about her. Yes, it might even be the woman he had tried to make friends with, before he was dragged away by the gang of Tealer men. It seemed possible that she had even physically objected to the gang of men removing the other men from the town. He went over to put more twigs on the little fire; it did not seem to help much with the warmth, but it did provide for some light to see, in his little shelter. Looking back at the woman, he was surprised to see her eyes open. Did that mean she had died or did it mean she was conscious? It had been many weeks since he had spoken a word. It took awhile, but he finally said a greeting toward the woman, alive or dead. After a long moment, she repeated his greeting. He brought a gourd of water to her lips, then some of the still fresh berries he had stashed away. She sipped the water, and seemed to savor the berries awhile, then her eyes shut and she lay back.

He had provided her a bit of comfort, so all this had been worth it, he decided.

He chose to go out and forage more, instead of having some of the stored food and water in here for breakfast. Opening the door, he discovered a thin layer of snow was all over everything outside. He put a little line of twigs along on his hearth, hoping the small fire would follow the twigs, stay lit while he was gone. He hurried out the door, shut it, and looked for twigs this time. He strove to gather them as far from his abode as possible, so there would be easier ones to find later in the winter, if the snow got deeper. He filled one his carrying gourds with twigs for the fire, and the other with edibles from the trees and bushes. He was always careful to not take all the fruit and nuts from any of the plants; more would be needed to seed the next generation of plants. Yet he could not stay out here long, in his thin clothing.

Arriving back at his abode, ready for anything including another person to bury, he was very relieved to find the woman sitting next to the fire, having dragged herself out of the stretcher and was adding a few twigs to the fire. He brought the new supplies over, and put the gourd full of twigs handy to the hearth. The woman looked at him awhile, silent. Finally she said she recognized him, he was one of the men who had left months ago. She had liked him; he had brought her little gifts in effort to woo her. The gang of men did not bring gifts, they just wanted to mate her saying they were her only choice now.

But there was another man not one of the Tealer gang, and she and her ladyfriend had tried to mate with him. But the gang saw that, and had dragged the man away. But this time, she and her ladyfriend followed the gang men, and climbed in back of their vehicle to see what was going on. When, after hours of riding, they arrived at the top of the cliff, and saw the gang was about to throw their favored man off the cliff, the two women had attacked the gang men; there were only two of them, since the captive man had been rendered unconscious and wrists tied together. But the Tealer gang members were tough, and fought off the women and threw the man off the cliff. The two women jumped on the two gang men, they yelled and struggled and somehow all had fallen off the cliff. She asked, how were the others.

All were dead, he had to tell her, and she alive only because she had landed on top of them. She was quiet a long time, then asked why he was not wearing warmer clothes. He said these were the clothes he was wearing when they threw him off the cliff. She said there were two gang men out there with warm clothes that they no longer needed; he ought to go get them and bring them here. And if he could, also bring the other woman's belongings here too, after burying her.

It made sense to him, but he was not in the mood to be going out in the cold and robbing the dead. Then he remembered seeing that one of the gangsters had been carrying something stolen from him before tossing him down here; he ought to at least go get it back. As he slowly went out the door, the woman repeated the request for all the warm clothing, woman's too. It was going to be very hard to survive here, and they needed all the resources possible.

3 UNKNOWINGLY LOVING

The next morning, the woman seemed to have a fever and was barely conscious. He piled the other woman's clothes atop her for warmth, and got her to drink a lot of water, and she ate a few nuts and berries. But then she lay back down and went unconscious again.

He fed the fire a bit more twigs than needed to stay lit, a little more warmth was needed by the woman. He needed to go get a lot more twigs for the fire, so out he went, going farther to gather the combustibles, as he could easily find his way back by his tracks in the snow. However, by the time his arms were full of firewood and headed back, the falling snow was starting to cover his tracks. He had to use the more familiar landmarks to find his abode at the end of the trip. He dumped most of the firewood outside the door, before going inside.

She was sitting up again, and helping herself to water and fruit, closer to the fire now. She was silent, eating, wincing at times when moving the broken limbs. Finally she asked if he enjoyed mating with her while she was unconscious. was she nice? After a moment's thought, he said he had not tried to mate with her. She had not agreed to be his mate, and besides, she was hurting and might be more injured by any such movement of her limbs. He was thinking that this was very unromantic, but she had brought the subject up. She was quiet a long time, then said he was welcome to mate with her anytime he wanted to. Her name was Lorimorning, what was his name? Burtevertree, he said.

It was looking like he was not fully doomed to the life of a hermit after all. Yet the woman clearly was fragile, needed much help to recover. The broken arm and leg would take a long time to heal, and she had other bruises, maybe other internal injuries. Plus a lump on her head; that might be why she was saying those things. When she got her senses back no doubt she would not be interested in mating with him. As if reading his mind, her eyes raised and looked into his eyes briefly as she smiled. Then the exhaustion overtook her again and she slumped back onto the leafy floor of his abode. He pulled the extra clothing over her, and added leaves for insulation, and propped her head up to a more comfortable position. Going out to gather more wood and food, the barely opened door showed that snow was falling heavily, already piled high all over here, a hand width's or more. He shut the door, and went over to the hearth, set the twigs to a minimum to keep burning for a few hours, then pulled some leaves over himself, and fell sleep.

He awoke to find some of the dead men's winter clothes had been piled on top of him, the clothing articles within arm's reach of the woman. However, she appeared to be sleeping again. He went to toss the other men's clothing off himself, then realized how warm it was under them, and how cold it was not under them. However, he got up enough to put all but one of the pieces of clothing on top of the woman; she needed warmth more than he did right now. He was more weary than weary, and soon was asleep despite shivering a bit.

He awoke warm, a nice feeling. Then he felt the sticks of a splint; the woman was right next to him and they both were covered by the extra clothing. The little hearth fire had been replenished, no need to get up into the cold. It had been a long time since he felt warm, and this was a fine warm. He was very careful to not bump the woman's splinted arm, then he fell back asleep.

There was no sunlight the next morning, but the little fire in the hearth was keeping the chimney path up through what seemed to be a thick snowpack on top of their little home. Lorimorning's fever seemed to have faded away, and she was moving around a bit, being careful of the injured arm and leg. She said she had some requests of him, one was to bring more fruit and nuts within reach of her good arm, and the other was for him to stay close to her to keep her warm day or night. When she repeated the request for him to mate her often, he said he did not know how to do that without damaging her broken leg. She paused awhile then said with another smile that when the leg was healed enough, he was going to have to mate with her twice as often to make up for lost time. She was already with child, but she hoped they could enjoy each other anyway.

Indeed, his life of a hermit seemed to have ended and a much better life had come forth. Yet she was clearly fragile, and he could tell that she was not feeling very well. When she asked for some hot soup, spoken with a bit of a slur, he knew she was out of it; when he replied that they did not have a pail in which to heat soup, nor anything from which to make soup, she merely reached over with her good arm and said that then would he please hold her close, that would do for now. And that indeed seemed a healing thing for her, and for him too.

By mid-afternoon they both were sitting up and feeling much better. He was starting to realize that his already meager winter stores of seeds and nuts that he had been able to gather, were going to be even less for two people, including one who was needing extra nourishment to rebuild damaged bone and tissue. At least the small collection of berries and fruit were probably going to last longer in the cold, and that would help them a bit longer than expected.

Well, he had survived this long by taking on one problem at a time, and longer term food was going to be solved similarly, he hoped.

Lorimorning asked about what work he had done in the town,

and then went on to say that most of the town's women had found that life was tolerable for them by the occasional mating demands by the Tealer gang men. But she would rather have had a man of her own who could also help her with her projects.

But, like what had happened to Bertevertree, any man in town who had stopped agreeing to be celibate as part of the town's rules, the other men who tried to become friendly with Lorimorning became stalked by the Tealer gang men and then would vanish, no one knew where. Now she new. She showed a bit of anger at the gang men and was glad that two of them were down off the cliff alongside the men they had captured and tossed off before. She was also sad for the very many men who had perished as victims of the town gang Tealer men, and sad for her lady-friend who had also perished in the event.

Changing the subject, Bertevertree asked what were her projects in town that she wanted a man's help doing. She was a seamstress, making many kinds of clothing, and had probably made the clothing they had in here now. The leather jackets and boots were hard to sew, and a man could help with that part, she thought. But she had always done it herself, lacking a man's help. But now she had no needle and thread, no bolts of cloth or skins from the hunt or farmer's livestock, with which to make clothing.

But she liked to make things with her hands; surely she could make things out of the resources they had here. Perhaps make baskets for food storage, for one kind of thing; the gourds were nice but would not hold much. He asked if she could make a carrying sling for hauling firewood; she said she would think about how to do that. Perhaps they could make baskets and firewood slings together somehow, her one good arm and his two, working together. This seemed complicated to him but also sounded like something nice to be doing with her. After all, he needed to learn to not live like a hermit anymore. And they would need all the skills of both of them, if they were going to survive very long in all this.

When he saw that she was rubbing one of his cutting rocks sideways against another cutting rock, she said she was sharpening them together. It looked like that was going to take a long time to do, but she said she needed something to do. And besides, she needed better cutting tools to make a couple bows and arrows; she had always gone hunting for the small animals that lived in the woods outside of town, to replenish her food supplies at times; being a single woman on her own resources, even in town. The money she was paid for making clothing, was controlled by the business people, and they paid her as little as possible, so she had to augment her nutrition by hunting. She said she was fairly skilled at archery. And she needed a bow and some arrows to get food that way.

He said he had not seen any animals while he had been down here. She said that there had to be animals to eat the berries and fruit, and distribute the seeds for the plants, so they must be in the area. As winter was approaching, the little animals probably had already stored up winter supplies and had retired to their winter homes before Bertevertree had arrived. He commented that he did not like the idea of using a bow and arrow on little animals but she said she had no problem doing that, and the animal skins could be used for making clothing and other items. However, having a broken arm did not work for archery. And a broken leg did not work for going hunting, either.

Neither of them could remember how long it took to mend a broken bone. The doctor in the town did the fixing of broken bones and such, but it was rare that anyone had such a major injury in town. Lorimorning asked him to carefully examine his emergency repairs to her broken arm and leg. He said the shin bone had not broken through the skin, and looked maybe in the correct joining together again, but her upper arm bone had punched through the skin, and so the splint seemed to be holding that bone together in about the correct position, but the flesh wound was looking a bit festered. She washed the caked blood off the wound, said she needed an herb to place on the wound for it to heal and keep her alive. She was willing to attempt to put extra clothing on and crawl outside and dig in the snow for the herb, but he said he would go look for it, but what kind of plant was it? She described it in terms of equal dimensions of specific fingers of hers, finger length stems, little round leaves. It was the leaves she needed.

4   PARTNER MAKES WORK WITH LOVE

Covering Lorimorning up carefully with the spare clothing there, without touching the arm wound that was freshly washed, Bertevertree pushed open the door of his little underground hut, pushing the snow aside. Snow was not falling now; he cleared snow away from the door and around its edges, so as to be able to find it easier, if the snow started falling again while he was out looking for the herb she needed. She had said that the herb tended to grow under a kind of tree that did not lose its leaves in wintertime, a tree that had long needles instead of leaves.

Standing up in the snow, he looked around; all the leaf trees had lost their leaves, but he now could see some that were different. It was difficult walking through the deep snow, but he cleared the snow off of a branch of each tree that he passed by on the way there, to make it easier to find his way back.

Arriving at the nearest still-green type tree, he dug down around its base. He broke off some pieces of each kind of plant he could find there, put them in a carrying gourd; added some of the tree's leaf-needles too as she had said she might be able to use them for her crafts-work.

He trudged back home, stepping in the tracks he had made on the way to the tree, easier than making fresh tracks. Back inside their hut, Lorimorning sorted through the various kinds of bits of plants that he had brought back, then handed him one of the bits of leaf and twig, and asked him to bring back a whole gourd full of those, but be sure to leave the main part of the plant intact so it can grow back easily next spring. She also handed him the sample of another kind of herb, asking him to bring some of them back too; they could be made into a medicinal tea. And while he was out there, could he please make a trip over to the base of the cliff where they had fallen, and see if he could find the side bag and its strap that one of the gang men had been carrying and had probably fallen off the cliff with them; the bag's strap could be used to make a sling for her arm, and the bag itself might have something useful in it too. And before he left, would he please bring some of the pile of firewood he had set outside the door, set it inside near the hearth.

As he trudged back to the still-green tree where the herbs were located, he was thinking that the life of not being a hermit was a lot harder than being a hermit. But it also was lots more interesting, too. And she could make lots of things that he could not make by himself. Still, he could be in his warm hut instead of trudging out here in the cold, and then digging in the snow with his bare hands, to find bits of plants that might be under the snow.

It took hours for him to find enough of the herb to fill the gourd, while sparing the main part of each plant too. He had also found a few handfuls of the tea leaf plant she wanted. The cliff was easily seen from there, so he set out making a fresh path through the snow from the green tree to there, instead of making a path from the base of the cliff to his home. When he got to the cliff, the area had changed some; like the other areas, the leaves had all fallen off the trees and bushes in the area; and, snagged in a short tree, he saw what must be the handbag with its strap caught on a tree limb, now visible with the leaves gone. He retrieved the bag and straps; at the edge of the cliff wall, he had already gotten a skill for finding useful shapes of rock and he broke off a flat piece from the rocky wall, to add to the size of their hearth. He then stepped back through the holes in the snow he had made, retracing his steps first to the herb-sheltering tree then from there to his home. He was quite tired by the time he was back inside; she quickly put more firewood on the hearth and told him to warm his hands there by the little fire.

She thanked him for the gourd full of leaves for her wound's poultice, and for the tea leaves, She offered him a tea leaf, warning that it would be bitter and would taste better when they could heat water and make a real tea from the leaves, but for now, eating a few leaves would be helpful. He found indeed the leaf was very bitter; but soon he experienced a bit of increased mental clarity.

Watching her, admiring her industriousness, as she unhooked the strap from the late Tealer gang man's side handbag, and looped it around her shoulder and under the broken forearm's splint. With the arm thus stabilized, then she could use that hand to help a little with the hand on the good arm to do things. Then she looked in the bag itself; it was made of leather, and she remembered making it, and that the request had been to make a hidden pocket inside the bag. Soon she had the items spread out in an array for them both to evaluate; the hidden pocket had held some money, not useful right now but maybe later. More useful were a small straight blade knife and a larger folding knife, a fork and spoon, and a metal cup.

There also were a couple short sections of rope, like the rope that he had been bound with as he found himself at the base of the cliff. Rope was potentially useful for making a sling for carrying firewood; and one piece of rope she took apart its twisted strands; the strands could be used for making the bowstrings, and also generally for tying and sewing things. She asked him to go out and clean off the knives, cup and eating utensils with snow, preferably snow a little ways from their abode. Then when he brought them back inside, she carefully heated each metal item up very hot in their little fire, to finish removing any pathogens the gang members might have been harboring. She had always thought the tough Tealer gang men looked a little sick and wondered if that was why they acted so violently.

Another object in the handbag was not familiar to her. Handing it to him, she asked what it was useful for; it was a fist-sized complex metal object with a crank handle on it. He twisted on the crank handle, and discovered that it lit a small bulb on the side of the object; it was a kind of flashlight.

The town had larger ones, which the men took turns cranking on at night, and the associated lightbulbs provided some light at night during special events. But he remembered an even more important use for such a device. He rummaged among the smaller stuff from the handbag and found some short wires and metal strips. He disconnected the light bulb, and ran wires from its the bulb's connector to a pair of metal strips, and asked Lorimorning to hold one of the metal strips in each hand, wetted with a bit of melted snow. He then began to crank on the little hand-generator's handle; she said she could feel a mild current while he cranked on the handle. He cranked on the handle for many minutes, until too tired to do more for now. Microbes had little tolerance for the small electrical current, but it did not bother multi-cell creatures like people, he said.

Then she resumed her tedious separation out of the herbal leaves for making the poultice; she had no mortar and pestle nor bandage cloth with which to soak the herbal juices for wrapping the wound; it would not be ready until tomorrow; and they both were much too tired.

But the next morning Lorimorning exclaimed that the wound on her arm had already lost its redness and much of the pain and swelling was already gone. He again explained that the small currents from the little hand generator were sometimes able to dispose of the pathogens that caused infections like that, and indeed seemed to be doing so now. After their little breakfast meal, he again cranked for many minutes while she held the metal strips in each hand, feeling the small electrical current that went from hand to hand, going past the site of the broken bone and damaged muscle and skin on the way. Afterwards, she was less intent on preparing the poultice; she made it into a paste, and painted it over the directly damaged skin areas, instead of all over the upper arm. That way she could save some of the herbal material in reserve for future emergencies, she said. But later in the day she was insistent that he crank on the little generator awhile more; she was feeling lots better in other areas too, not just the broken arm. Even her broken leg felt better now, she declared. She took back the little generator and associated wires and metal strips, and its lightbulb, carefully stashing it as if a real treasure that belonged to her. She gave him the large folding knife, and kept the straight blade knife for herself; it would be very helpful in craft work. And Burtevertree could take the larger knife and go find a couple of tree branches that were of proper shape to make a crutch for her, and please go do that now; it would take her a long time to make the crutch even after he brought the pieces to her, so the sooner starting the better.

Out searching for specially sized and shaped tree branches, he was again pondering on that he had indeed asked for this care-taking duty, giving up the independent life of a hermit, by deciding to nurse her back to health. It took little effort for him to decide it was a very good trade, even as he made new step-holes in the deep snow, from tree to tree searching for proper branches, while also keeping track of his location. It took hours, but eventually he was back inside their home, handed her the tree branches, and waited to see if she declared they were useful for more than firewood. She clearly was not really happy with the pieces he brought back, but then said she would find a way to make them work, along with some pieces from their firewood pile.

5 HEALING AND COMPREHENDING

Lorimorning soon had another project for him. She wanted another room added to their abode, and she gestured where it needed to be made. It needed to be high enough so that a person could stand up and walk around in it, unlike their current abode, which was high enough to sit in but not to stand up in. The new room would enable her to get practice with the crutch, and to recondition her muscles for walking. The new room would also have two seating surfaces made in the walls for sitting like in a chair. It also would have a large bin along one wall, for storage of firewood and building materials, rocks. He would need to go above ground, scrape away the snow from above the area, putting the snow to partially shield from the prevailing breeze, then start digging out the packed leaves. He would have to have it fully built and roofed over before he then broke through the separation to re-enter their warm living area.

He started on the project early the next morning, clearing the snow. The top layer of leaves were all that were frozen; his makeshift hoe worked well for removing them. Occasionally he went back inside their home to warm up and to have a meal with her. One time he asked what she was doing, ever busy, mostly rubbing rocks together. She held up one of the double-fist-sized rocks, that now had been smoothy rounded on its outside, and she was tediously wearing away the inside so as to make it into a small bowl. She said it would be a cooking pot someday. It was slow going, rubbing the rocks together, but clearly she was making progress.

He also built a ramp down into the ever deeper hole, unsure that he would keep it as a secondary exit or not. Two exits from an abode seemed wise, but doorways were hard to keep sealed. By the time he had roughed out the digging of the new room, he had decided to keep the ramp as a secondary exit, but for now to roof over the ramp and seal it up. That way would minimize heat loss yet still be easy to open up later.

The new room was long and narrow, to minimize the length of tree branches needed to span the roofing. He also prepared an area for another hearth and chimney, although he had no more gourds for chimney tubing nor rocks for the floor of the hearth and back-wall; at least there was a place for them to be put later. They would probably need to use a hearth down here anyway, otherwise it would be too cold here. In fact, moving the existing gourds and hearth stones down here seemed the way to go, but would need to be approved by Lorimorning, since she would need to do the cooking using her stone cooking pot, eventually. The new hearth would be twice as big as the existing one, which had originally been intended mostly to keep a small fire lit and not for cooking. He also built it so the leaf insulation in the roof was twice as thick as in his hurriedly built original room. This one was being built better, with intent for long term housing for two people.

Three days later he had it built, even the top was filled with packed leaves and the earlier removed snow was put back on top. The only way to get into it now was to dig through from their existing room. Lorimorning watched intently as he dug through the wall, hauled leaves out their door, dug some more. He had put roof beam branches right on the location of the eventual access ramp from the old room, but had not removed the material where the tunnel would be; he dug up to the underside of that roofed over area and that was to be the ceiling of this access hallway ramp. The difference in floor level was considerable, and had resulted in a further distance between the rooms than originally envisioned, but she would need a gentle sloping ramp to get between the rooms.

Finally the tunnel broke through to the new space, but it was very dark in there. And there was no ventilation yet, so they dare not have a fire going in there. They discussed moving the hearth and gourd chimney into the new room; she said it would be better to build a new one with new materials. All made of stone, including the chimney. For now, she took the initiative, dragging herself down the ramp, carrying a small torch made of small branches to light the way. She got down into the new room with her little light, looked around, said it looked great. And yes too cold to start living there without a fireplace and a controlled air inlet.

She insisted that he use the little generator while she held the metal strips to its output; she was sure it was helping her a lot. Her arm had begun to heal up even faster than her leg was doing, and it had not broken through the skin. The infection was going away fast, and she had only made the poultice once for her arm wound; she felt the generator was the main thing helping her recover right now, along with the food and his tender care.

He got into a discussion with her, musing his former acceptance of life as a hermit from then on. She declared that his life as a hermit was over, she would make sure he would not lack woman's companionship. He did like her, correct? she added, a bit uncertainly. Oh yes he replied, he could not do without her now. And yes she had brought more work into his life, along with even more joy.

Winter was getting colder. Neither knew how deep the cold snow would get, nor how long it would last. Burtevertree asked her about the journey she and her girlfriend took, hiding in the back of the vehicle that the two gang men were using to take away her friend's boyfriend. "The trip took a long time. It got dark and then daylight when the vehicle stopped and then we two women peered out at what was happening." They saw the two gang-men carrying her friend's boyfriend. There was a visible edge of a cliff. She and her friend suddenly realized that the gang-men pair intended to throw her friend's limp boyfriend off the cliff. That was when they decided to go try to save the man from being thrown off the cliff, and ran over to try to protect him, just as he was being thrown off. And you know the rest of the story."

He thought about that awhile, then said it did not make any sense to him. Yet probably the same thing had been done to me. Only the bush clinging to the cliff had saved his life, the bush he had now replanted outside their home.

She brought his musings back to the subject. She had thought about it all a lot. She had seen many things over the years in the town, as she became fertile and thus of interest to the men. The town had a rules teaching building, where everybody was required to visit once a week. While there, the Tealer town leaders told of an invisible ruler who would punish those who disobeyed the rules. And the most important rule was to obey the Tealer town leaders' invisible entity. And the second rule was part of that, all men had to be celibate, leaving the women of the town alone. Only the chosen ones of the thirty Tealer leaders group were allowed to be friendly with the women of the town. Any man seen trying to be friendly with any woman was subject to the terrible wrath of the invisible ruler who watched all and sees all, and rules mightily.

But what she herself had seen, was that there were a small group of men who declared to be the invisible ruler's chosen ones, who visited the women and provided offspring thereby. She herself had already provided one such offspring, who was taken away by the rules leaders, for their purposes; and she was now again with child by them. But she did not really like any of the chosen ones, the men who were the Tealer gang men of Burtevertree's awareness. Many of the town's women liked to compete for the favors of the Tealer town leaders, but she and her girlfriend, who had a secret lover that was not of the chosen men of the rules group, felt that maybe there was something not fully truthful going on.

And when they fortunately happened to observe the kidnapping of her friend's boyfriend by two members of the "chosen ones" the thirty dominant Tealer gang-men, they had immediately decided to find out what was really going on. And that had resulted in the death of her girlfriend, perhaps on impact with her boyfriend as they hit the rocky bottom of the cliff. But they had also dragged down two of the gang men with them; and the pile had saved Lorimorning's life enough that Burtevertree could save her.

This seemed to fit in with what he knew from his life in the town. The rules leaders proclaimed an invisible ruler that they served, an invincible ruler who saw everything all the people did. A ruler who destroyed all men who disobeyed the rule of them being celibate. Only the Chosen Ones of the rules group were allowed to visit the women of the town when they were in their fertile time. Maybe it involved a reproduction deception activity. But there was still the factor of the invisible ruler that saw all, and provided the chosen ones with knowledge of who was disobeying and perhaps might mate with some woman of the town.

Surely that invisible all-knowing ruler would realize that the vehicle had not returned from doing a physically real abduction and disposal of a non-celibate man. And so there would be another vehicle come out, and then find the missing vehicle up on top of the cliff above them. And they might surmise that something had gone wrong and all had gone over the cliff; the only way the vehicle could still be there, the two chosen-ones gang-men not returning, and two women also missing from town. The all-seeing were likely to come looking to find out what happened. And they might find Bertevertree and Lorimorning living closely, down here.

She murmured as she snuggled with him, that the way down here was fast but hazardous, and the way back up unknown. He replied that cliffs have finite expanses, and easy ways down and up surely existed. She murmured that not in the snow; be closer with her now.

6   INVISIBLE MAGNETIC FIELDS

The woman was very practical, Burtevertree decided. And she was very skilled at making things. She also seemed to understand the doings of people a lot better than he did. But most importantly, she was very friendly to him, so close each night now, his hopes of long ago fulfilled. Life was good. Finally.

But he recalled the implication of their conversation of last night while snuggling to keep each other warm and comforted. It suggested that the vehicle up on top of the cliff, would attract the gang-men to come down here to see what had happened. Maybe not until spring, when the snows were gone. Assuming that they had not already come there and found the empty vehicle.

He replied that the existence of the gang men doing the disposal of men who were not their members, but were not willing to be celibate, indicated it was all a fake. She replied that no, there really was an invisible entity that saw all. But it would tell all to whoever asked of it. The Tealer gang-men, the self-proclaimed chosen ones, had been told of that function, and used it to find which women were not just breeding with the gang men, and then to find which of the townsmen were not being celibate. Then after a moment, he asked her if she could ask the invisible see-all entity if the vehicle were still atop the cliff.

She was quiet awhile, and said the vehicle was indeed still up there. And it had not been visited by any others. Furthermore, there were no plans for the gang-men to return the the cliff; they were worried about why their Chosen Ones gang men had not returned; maybe their invisible ruler was upset with them? And from the past, they knew that it was snowy way over here, no place to travel until after the spring had arrived.

But she continued, that the part that worried her most, was that the invisible see-all would also be able to see through Burtevertree's eyes, and thus would know of what was happening here, perhaps even right now. She did not care; she wanted to love in the moment, and leave the nastiness of others' reproductive rivalry control to some other time. The see-all tell-all did not seem to have anything to do with ruling other people, but knowing how to access that knowledge enabled certain kinds of clever bully men to trick others into believing those men had special powers assisted by a powerful invisible entity. The town's gang-men were of that kind of men, particularly their leaders; she had at times been requested to be in a group of the town's women who the gang-men demanded that the women all imagine a specific thing happening in the near future, all the women at the same time, and to stir up a desire that it happen. The gang-men said this would help communicate it to the powerful ruler who the gang-men served, and then the powerful invisible ruler would make it happen. And she said it usually did happen; it worked. But in her experience, it seemed more that it was the women's group common-vision that was what brought forth the requested near-future event. It did not matter to the women; it was a way for them to get together, and to win the special attention of the gang-men, more than just being breeders for them. It all worked well for everybody, except for those who met misfortune when the group-visions of the women happened, and the envisioned events usually were for non-gang-men to lose something to one or more of the gang-men, such as in sports or business competition.

He replied that it sounded a lot like magic in some aspects. She said that no, in this case, it clearly was the agenda of the gang-men that was being manifested. The gang-men merely pretended it was an invisible powerful man who liked the gang-men and wanted their exclusive reproduction to happen, along with their business dealings to preferentially happen; this diverted the attention of the townspeople from realizing that it was just a ruse by the gang-men who were using a normal aspect of reality but keeping it a secret from others, thus it looked mysterious.

He added that it was a bit like when the little hand-crank flashlight was invented, there were some enterprising guys who learned the means of making the device from the inventor and then killed him; and then they proclaimed that the device was a gift of an invisible supreme entity that favored those guys by giving them the means to make and sell the devices. But in time those who were carefully studying and experimentally manipulating the physical world had also discovered electricity and how a moving magnet generated current in a nearby conductor, and that was what made the little hand generator flashlight work.

There had been much conflict and hard feelings from the men who claimed the device was given to them by the invisible supreme entity for their exclusive business use, attempting to make the people think that the scientists and engineers were pawns of a rival invisible entity who was trying to cause the downfall of everybody and take over control of the town.

A court of law was convened to make some judgment upon the rival entity's science-minded folks, and the focus was on the demonstration that it could be proven that the magnet did not touch the conductive wires, yet the wires had current created in them that lit the light bulb of the light. It was an invisible entity that was invoked that went between the magnet and the wires; this was easily proven by a demonstration setup, there was no physical contact between the moving magnet and the wires, and a brave person could even put his hand in the space between the moving magnet and the coil of wires, and not feel anything going through the space between the magnet and the coil of wires. It had to be an invisible entity that was being invoked, proven by the demonstration.

However, the court of judgement was wise enough to proclaim that it clearly was an invisible entity that obeyed any builder of such a device, not just obey the group who proclaimed themselves the sole rightful makers and sellers of the device, granted special powers by an invisible ruler of everything. It was clear to the court that the invisible entity that passed between moving magnet and coil of wires, obeyed anybody who built such a mechanism; it was one of the physical laws, like the invisible entity that pulled everything down toward the ground, seemingly without touching them; and the invisible entity clearly had no interest in being rulers of men giving special status to some of the men thereby. The pull toward the ground worked for everybody, not just the elite men. And similarly the invisible entity that passed between the magnet and the coil of wires, seemed to have no interest whatsoever in ruling people.

Burtevertree believed that there was an entity who had made all of the world and even the invisible pull toward the ground and the energy leap from moving magnet to wire coils, among other parts of the creation. But that entity did not have any preference for some gang of men over other men; craving to be being a ruler of others seemed to be a quirk of some strains of men, not of the supreme maker of everyone's existence and all the world.

She filled in that the invisible means for seeing things out of range of the physical eyes, was just like the invisible entity that pulled everything toward the ground and that spanned between moving magnet and wires. Yet it was not just wishful thinking that built the hand-crank magnet, cranked coil of wires and light bulb that could light up the night; it took a lot of physically modifying of the stuff of the world to build such a device.

The invisible connection between her and the top of the cliff to see if the vehicle were still there, was equally something built, and apparently was built in each human, just like hands and feet and eyes were built into each person. But a person does not walk without learning to walk; we could always just crawl around on hands and knees instead. But learning how to stand up and walk and run enables a person to go much farther and faster than if just limited to crawling on the ground. And, some people could walk and run a bit faster than other people, if that made much difference.

He explored the concept that the ways people thought, were not all the same. There were a few kinds of viewpoints, and the kind of viewpoint characterized the individual person. One kind of viewpoint was that there was an implicit hierarchy among people, among all things too. There was a place in that hierarchy where all individual men were placed. All that mattered was who was boss of whom. The men could strive to show they were better than the next person above them in the hierarchy, and if successful, they traded places, the one person going lower in the hierarchy and the other going higher. And the only way to get to the top of the hierarchy was to have contests with the next higher person in the hierarchy, one at a time climbing the ladder, but never jumping from one rung to another.

And in such a hierarchy there often would be a limited few up near the top of the hierarchy who acted together to help any of them being contested by the person below them, and so no individual could withstand the combined efforts of the layer of men just above them. This then preserved the top layers of the hierarchy from risk of being supplanted by those striving below them. And those whose minds worked in the hierarchical vision way, assumed all people existed only in the hierarchy, and any man trying to get far ahead would be considered out of place and thus a very unwanted person, to be scorned, particularly by the women who had been taught to prefer men higher in the hierarchy.

But the picture of the universe as a hierarchy was only one kind of viewpoint. Many other people saw the universe from different perspectives. Some of the perspectives acknowledged the existence of other perspectives, but a few of the perspectives considered the hierarchical viewpoint the only valid perspective, and so all those who did not share that perspective were considered defective, out of place, in some way.

7   FINDING A CAVE

As they finally fell asleep, their conversation had finished making a bit more of their consensus reality that would enable their coordination better in the future.

Awakening the next morning, it was increasingly cold out there, much nicer snuggled in here together, but there were needs to be freshened up and to become nourished. So they arose and prepared for the day.

After breakfast, she insisted that he first help her get down into the lower room, bringing the crutch with them. He would help her stand up, supported partially by a wall, and give her the crutch. Then in the darkness he would crank on the hand generator flashlight, enabling them to see, as she learned to adjust to supporting weight using the crutch. It fit under the shoulder of her non-broken arm; the broken arm was in the sling and its hand was able to hold things a bit. They both tired of the activity in only a couple minutes, she with the effort of long-unused muscles trying to cope with standing up and taking a step, and he tired of cranking on the crank generating light. She asked him to stop cranking, carefully reach to her and lightly hold her as they walked a few steps together in the dark, to the ramp which led up into their warm room with its small flickering fire on the hearth. Then he helped her gently back to the awkward crawl mode she had adopted to move around. She asked that they do that several times each day, to help her get stronger again. It also enabled a little compression of the break of her shinbone, and she thought that would help it grow back together better, a bit at a time.

She was ever practicing moving her broken arm that was in a sling, yet ever careful to not exceed the capacity of the healing areas to cope. She insisted that he daily apply the electricity from the hand-crank device to provide the small current that kept the infection from returning, and enabled the bone to grow together faster. They occasionally set it up so the current would have to flow through the broken leg, in hopes that would speed up its healing too.

Pushing open the door, they found it had snowed again. He dug snow away from the door, packing the snow into an arch over the doorway. The snow was falling heavier all the time, so he extended the packed snow arch covered path to cover above where they had added the new room below, and then he dug down the side of the room for a chimney for a new fireplace. The archway had become a tunnel which supported the newly falling snow.

The making of the snow tunnel became an outdoor activity for him, and he slowly built it along the ground toward where there had been sources of seeds and nuts nearby, saved for a time like this. He was careful to not take all the plants, nor all of a plant's seeds, but leave enough that the plants could quickly thrive in spring. When he returned to their home with plentiful seeds and nuts and even some frozen fruit, Lorimorning was overjoyed at the new food.

The snow was still falling two weeks later, and Lorimorning was often out on her crutch, inside the archway snow tunnel at least near the doorway of their home. Burtevertree was ranging further out with his arched snow tunnel building, and had now reached the nearest face of the cliff wall. He then built the snow arch along the face of the cliff a few yards in each direction, and collected favored rock shards for building the hearth in the lower room of their home.

He had found a large crack in the face of the cliff; curious about it, he then used packed snow to build a series of steps up the face of the cliff, along that crack, which seemed to have a brush-filled shelf of some kind up there, out of reach from the ground without the packed snow steps. A ladder could be made, perhaps to reach there, if there were something interesting enough up there. He dug through the bushes and small trees behind the ones in front, increasingly curious about what was further behind. And indeed he found that the crack into the face of the cliff had formed a cave as if from water seeping down; he was able to crawl into the cave after unblocking the entrance from vegetation and fallen rocks. Inside the cave, it seemed to get larger the further it went, but he could not see far using only the light from the small entrance.

With some excitement, he returned through the long snow tunnel to greet Lorimorning, who was still doing her contrived exercises near the front of their home. She listened to his description, then asked him to help her back inside, she was getting cold and tired out there; but then to take the hand crank light and go look a bit further into the cave, gather more information about it. She also mentioned a worry that when all this snow would be melting in springtime, it might flood their home here, and an alternate place to stay until the water went down could become very helpful; so quick, go and learn more about it, being careful.

He knew it was late afternoon by the time he had reached the cave; snow was still falling. He adjusted the branches that he had broken off so as to gain access to the cave's entrance, up over the top front of the cave, to catch the snow and roof over the area a bit. Then he crawled inside, and cranked on the generator light, followed the cave, which seemed to go deeper into the cliff getting wider and lower. Finally there was a pool of water that vanished into the darkness, but the walkway of the cave went past that low point, and began a steep upward slope, down through which a trickle of water flowed. Would it be filled with water when the snows above were rapidly melting, he wondered. Then he had to turn back, already tired of cranking on the generator; he did not want it to be dark and have to use the generator to find his way through the snow tunnel all the way home.

Warming himself at their little hearth back home, Lorimorning was eager to hear of his adventure. That the tunnel cavern might become flooded in spring seemed a lot like their current spring water worry. But neither had happened yet, and the leafy forest floor surely could soak up a lot of water without flooding the surface above. They might need to prepare a temporary above-ground shelter before spring, however.

He said that there was no sign of heavy water flow out through the cave opening in the face of the cliff wall, where the brush was. They clearly had grown there a long time and had not been washed out by a lot of flowing water. So it seemed likely there were at least some areas inside the front of the cave that could be made habitable. A ladder would need to be made to reach the entrance to the cave, for use when the snow steps were melted away. She thought that a ladder that could be raised, might be an advantage if threatened.

Finding firewood was difficult in the snow-covered terrain, and finding branches suitable for making a ladder seemed more needed for warmth as firewood right now. Still, he looked for possible long poles adequate for such a ladder, as he dug around in the snow the next morning. He mainly wanted to resume his mapping of the cave; Lorimorning did not want to give up the hand generator; she had contrived a way to send its gentle pulses through herself, flowing through both broken bone areas at the same time. She said the infection was completely gone in the arm, and in fact she felt healthier than she had in years. So bring the hand generator back soon, she asked, as he had headed out with it in his pocket.

He left the few bits of firewood and edibles he had gathered on the way to the face of the cliff, at the bottom of the steps he had built into a ramp to reach the entrance to the cave. He kept one stick for possible use in prodding things, however; since there might be other creatures that had prior claim on the cave as a shelter, even though he had not seen any indication of that yesterday.

There were only a few areas where he had to stoop as he walked along the cave tunnel, past the large underground pond from where apparently water flowed out somewhere beyond the reach of his hand-crank light, and then walking past the furthest travel he had done yesterday. There were no side corridors, just the gentle slope upwards, apparently following the major crack up through the wall of the cliff. He also attempted to count his steps as a measure of distance, but the uneven path made for uneven distances among the steps he took.

Then light ahead, and crawling up a collapsed area, he was outside again, along the side of a small outcropping, but clearly now on top of the cliff. Realizing that he needed to not leave indication of a pathway for inquisitive townspeople of hostile intent, he looked around for a vehicle; he had been brought there knocked unconscious and thrown off the side of the cliff, so there was no familiarity to the view. But there clearly was a snow-covered vehicle about a hundred yards away. If he made a path through the deep snow to explore the vehicle, the path could be used by others seeking cause of the vehicle not returning to town, and thus discover he and Lorimorning, perhaps even when they were asleep. Besides, they were almost defenseless; Lorimorning had made a simple archery set for hunting small animals, was about their only defense. The small arrows probably would not kill people but it might hurt enough to make them go away. But the Tealers no doubt would have real weapons if they were hunting survivors of their disposal activities.

8   TRUCK AND JUNK

Back home that evening, he handed the hand generator to Lorimorning, and while she used it to run current through her injured arm and opposite side broken leg, she had lots of questions about the finding of a vehicle up there. She was sure it would be the one that she and her friend had stowed away on while it was taking her friend's boyfriend to throw him off the cliff.

She thought about the vehicle, describing it as much as she could remember, to Burtevertree, as he rested by the fire, munching seeds and nuts. She said it was some kind of utility truck, as the two women had hidden inside the back area of the truck. The interior seemed to have stowage areas, and in fact it was about packed with stuff, most of it apparently just thrown in, the place not intended for human occupancy. There must be a large area up front for carrying people, awake or not. She thought there would be lots of resources in the truck that they needed; if he could make a circuitous route through the snow to the truck, then throw the contents of the truck off the cliff, then return to the cavern, brushing away signs of his trip to the truck , it would be helpful. They then could go gather the items from the bottom of the cliff, some in winter and others after the snow melted.

So the next day, Burtevertree returned through the cavern, then waded through the deep snow over to the truck. It was right next to the edge of the cliff, apparently to make it easy to toss the victims over the side. From all the skeletons he had found down there, the truck had apparently hauled a lot of people here for disposal. Looking in the back of the truck, its doors still open apparently as left by the frantic women trying to rescue the latest victim, it indeed looked like a huge amount of stuff in there. Lots of electrical equipment, mainly, it seemed to him.

He got into the driver's seat, and checked to see if the engine would start. After a couple of attempts, the engine started up; he left the engine running so as to recharge the battery a bit. He got out and dug a path to the edge of the cliff, for tossing things over; then he realized it would be easier to just deliver the whole truck with its contents over the cliff. That way the stuff would remain in the back of the truck, easier to find than hunting all over in the snow and brush below. So he cleared a path from the front of the truck to the cliff's edge; it looked like a very long way down there to the bottom of the cliff. Leaving the door open, he got the truck moving, and he jumped out just before it went over the cliff. It made little noise from far below, the deep snow probably cushioning it too, a bit.

Peering over the side, he saw that the truck was on its side; he could not hear an engine running. Well, if people came looking in springtime, they would find no vehicle up here to point the way to his new home. But in case they came before all snow had melted, he then began to drag snow over to fill in where the truck had been, and its path over the cliff. He then backtracked his way to the cave's upper entrance, filling in his tracks as much as possible, even first digging out the compressed snow from where he had made the path. It was dusk by the time he got back to the upper entrance to the cave; and he was very tired. Inside the cave, he rested for awhile in the darkness, then started up the hand-crank flashlight, and made his way through the tunnel and then out through the snow-tunnel he had made, collapsing into his underground home.

Lorimorning spoon-fed him some warmed soup she had made in her stone cooking pot, and soon both were snuggled asleep.

By the next morning they both were full of questions about new opportunity and new risk, now that the truck was down here. By the many men's remains down below the cliff, in states from decomposition from maybe weeks to clearly many years bleached white, the abductions had been going on for a long time. Lorimorning thought back of the many times that it had been announced in the weekly all-town meeting that someone had chosen to go seek opportunity at a distant manufacturing town; she wondered why it was always the nice men who had been getting friendly, but then suddenly were gone and their departure was announced. And none came back. Since it was always the handsome helpful men who had decided to seek friendship with one of the women but then left her without a goodbye, Lorimorning had decided that the men who vanished were going to some far away town where perhaps men who were not of the town's leaders, were allowed to have a woman as mate, or none of the women in this town were good enough for the man, so he left town. That was what she thought about Burtevertree; he had been getting friendly with her and she wanted him and then he left without a goodbye, the town Tealer leaders announcing his decision to leave, a couple days after she had not seen him anymore.

So it could be that it was just the same two men and the same vehicle that always came to this place to dispose of men who did not want to be celibate anymore, and thus the men who led the town would have competition for the women who wanted to procreate. If it was only the same two men doing the disposals, then maybe no one else knew where this place was. The weather here was very different from that experienced in town, so it could be far away. It seemed possible that no one would come looking for the truck. And two more men missing would not be all that strange to the townspeople, but it sure would be noticed by the Tealer men who ruled the town. Clearly also there would be less competition among those who did electrical repair work, with this truck missing along with the men who had done that repair work.

For now, it seemed there was little to fear about their being discovered by the tough guys who were the leaders of the town. So contriving hidden pathways seemed maybe unnecessary as they planned their access to the truck's contents. But, the snow was so deep that it was about as easy to make a covered arch of compressed snow as the new path was made, as to just throw the snow over the top of the trench. And starting the new path would be easier starting from the nearest part of their existing trail system. Getting started on the task of building a snow tunnel over to the truck, did not seem so urgent, if the truck was likely to never be even sought by any passing on the road on top of the cliff.

They discussed what they had seen in the back of the truck; it seemed like electrical junk. Rigging up some lights in their home would be nice, and if they could contrive a hand crank generator to charge the truck's battery, they could have a small electrical system at home someday.

Then they remembered their guessing that when the snow melted, the water could get a bit deep all over here, and snow melt might even pour over the cliff to add to the water down here. Lorimorning pointed out the diversity of shrubs and trees of many heights, so the area probably was not submerged very deep for very long in spring.

But even a short while of being submerged could ruin the battery in the truck, and much of its electrical system. So the plan was to dig a snow tunnel toward the truck, as part of their gathering of frozen fruit, berries seeds and nuts, as well as some of the leafy edibles, always leaving enough for their fresh start in spring. And the thought that the cave was the place most likely to have areas not covered with water come springtime, so that would be where they needed to store electrical stuff from the truck.

Burtevertree was something of a mechanic too. With the new resource, he began to mentally explore possible options. Hauling the truck's big internal combustion engine to the cave was not possible, but if he could remove its small external combustion idler engine, maybe he could modify it to be a wood-fired engine to drive the generator from the truck.

The truck had come to a stop, tilted over on its side, with the fuel filler upward. So not likely that it would be losing gas rapidly. But fuel could be seeping from elsewhere in the fuel system, at that odd angle. It might be desirable to make an initial visit to the truck as soon as easily done.

Lorimorning wanted to show him something before he left, and help her a bit with it. Helping her up out of the doorway accessing the snow tunnel, he expected her to show that she could walk on crutches, but instead, she brought a cane she had made. A cane worked better, being used by the strong arm, which was on the side of the broken leg. But she was able to put some weight on her injured leg, helping the cane's support, and also she carefully removed the sling on her arm, keeping it slung over her shoulder however. She then carefully walked several yards down the tunnel, he close by in case she were to fall; but she managed the trip down the tunnel and back with dignity even if quite slowly. Helping her back down into their home, she asked him to let her use the hand crank generator to send the electrical signals through her injured arm and leg again, before he took it with him when going back to the cave. She was sure the small electrical currents were speeding up her healing and even the bone growing back together faster.

Burtevertree decided he did not need to go to the cave today; he instead would begin making the covered snow tunnel toward the truck site. And she could keep the generator for the next several days to speed her regeneration, too. It would take many days to reach the truck site, although he was not exactly sure of the shortest path there.

9 CHARGING BATTERIES

A couple days later his digging toward the truck area encountered a skeleton, so he knew he was getting close. He shifted the path around the skeleton; the frozen ground did not make for easy burial right now. He dug a hole up through the top of the snow, made a couple of steps packed in the snow to look over the top. Looking around, he realized that he had dug past the truck, assuming it is the large snow-covered thing not too far away. Backtracking a bit, he used the snow dug out of the diverted tunnel direction, to plug up the hole he had made in the snow, and to pack over the area where the skeleton was.

However, he encountered two more remains before bumping up against the truck. He dug around removing the snow from under the tilted up bottom-side of the truck; when the area was clear, he dug a smaller path to the other side, and from there, shoved the truck back fully upright. The cab of the truck was partly crushed and windshield smashed in, but it looked like the side windows were still intact; glass useful for windows at home looked feasible. The door that he had left open was a bit bent but enabled easy getting into the warped cab area, where there were tools scattered all over, and a toolbox soon found. He gathered up what tools he could find, and used a screwdriver to take off a door panel, and soon had the window in hand, and a pocket full of redundant tools. Leaving most of the tools there for taking the truck apart later, he headed back home.

Mornings became a routine of taking Lorimorning out for an increasingly lengthly walk, steadying her when needed, and then helping her exhausted self get back into their little underground home. Then he would leave her with the hand-crank generator that she increasingly used to help speed up her bodily healing, and headed out for the truck site.

Scavenging for useful items in the truck's cab, he felt a bit like a robber, then remembered that under the snow all around here, were hundreds of skeletons of men, who the owners of these truck items had killed by throwing them off the cliff down to smash on the rocks down here, so as to keep the men from competing with them for the affections of the town's women. Most of the men of the town were adequately tricked into celibacy by the men who ruled the town; but when a man just was too interested in getting closer to one of the town's women, he would instead supposedly choose to suddenly leave to go to another town, or so people were told. Now those hundreds of men who liked the women too much, were like ghosts down here where he worked, scavenging from the truck that probably had brought every one of those men here to their doom.

Still, sometimes the stuff seemed a little like someone else's property. For example, he had found a little box hidden under the driver's seat, that had a device that was very well crafted and of intricate design, but he had no idea of what it was for; he put it in the pile of things to take home.

Getting the little external combustion starter-idler engine pulled out was looking quite hard to do right now, so he dug around and got the back doors open to the truck. Lots of junk in there. He began to sort through the closer stuff, looking for useful things. The longer he worked at that task, the more he was realizing that it was indeed really junk. Very little that could be used to repair things. It more looked like the broken machinery and electrical items that they had replaced with new-bought equivalents. Perhaps this pile of junk was here to make people think that the owner of the truck knew how to fix things. The guys simply had sold people new things, and hid the junk equipment in here to conceal that the two men had not actually fixed anything.

Everything in the back of the truck was broken; worn out sometimes. Still, Burtevertree chose to spend a bit of time each day taking the broken things apart, and setting aside the screws and other pieces that looked like they would still work or be useful. Pieces of wire could be quite useful in making the planned electrical system in their home.

Yet he also wondered if their underground home would get totally flooded when all this snow melted; the water had to go somewhere. Any electrical system he put into their home, would get ruined by such flooding, even if relatively temporarily flooded. He would need to build the electrical system as something that was fairly portable, to be carried to the cave. The truck's battery would be a key item in such an electrical system; and that big battery was very heavy. Just hauling it in a hurry to the cave, looked like a big task. He had found a couple of portable lights, with batteries that were heavy, but apparently had been recharged off of the truck's electrical system.

He decided that the best way to go for now, was to haul the big truck battery up into the cave, taking some of the lights and wiring to go with it; he would count on eventually getting the little external combustion engine going to recharge that battery. The only generator was the big one that the truck's engine used to power its lights and recharge the truck battery, so he next made a project to remove that generator. Getting it out, it was not as heavy as was the truck battery. He collected window cranks, gears, and drive belts and metal scraps that looked like they could all be built into a hand-crank powered electrical generator, for recharging the truck battery and the two smaller portable work light's batteries. All the batteries were depleted now; he knew that batteries would become useless if left in such condition too long.

There were two hand trucks found in the back of the truck, and he chose to use one of them to haul his pile of stuff home, that looked like could be made into the generator for back home. Pulling the hand truck with its load of near-junk, he got home to realize that the better work area would be out in the snow tunnel archway in front of their door, so he left it there for the night.

The next morning, Lorimorning saw the pile of stuff outside their door, as they went on their usual walk to strengthen her ability to walk. When they returned, she asked to be brought back out here, after they had a meal inside, to watch him build the thing. He explained the urgency to get some electrical charge into these batteries as soon as possible; she suggested using their little hand-crank flashlight's output to do that. So they contrived a way to connect the little hand-crank generator to put current into the cells of one of the portable light's battery, charging each of the larger battery cells one by one, counting the same number of turns of the crank, so that they would have about equal charge on them.

When they had gone through hand-crank charging all 12 of the battery cells, they tested and found it did indeed light its light bulb again; they left it on less than a second, however, to conserve the bit of charge in the battery. They went through each of the cells of the battery once again, giving equal numbers of turns on the generator's hand crank. There, that was one battery that was functional.

She went back down into their home, and Burtevertree used the rest of the light of the day to make a quick trip to the truck, bringing back the other portable light.

Early the next day, Lorimorning insisted in going for their walk without her using the sling or cane. He brought those things along anyway; and before they got back home, she welcomed the sling for her arm, and the cane for her weak leg. Nonetheless, she had demonstrated to both of them, that she was getting able to get around by herself. She chatted about getting able to do archery again; she had made a bow and a few arrows; they needed some better protein in their nutrition.

But he pointed out that in all his gathering of fruit, nuts and seeds, he had seen no sign of there being any little animals eating any of them. The plants all seem to self-seed in their own vicinity, seeds only moved a little by the occasional small breeze. No animals were helping the plants spread their seed around. It looked like this area below the cliffs was actually fully ringed by such cliffs, so it was an isolated ecosystem. Possibly even small animals that were to fall off the high cliffs down into here, likely would suffer the same fate as the people did.

Lorimorning thoughtfully replied that it was possible, such a thing. When this planet was seeded by the seed-ships a great many decades ago, this sunken area would have gotten the same seeds as everywhere else did, and the subsequent seasons selected out the kinds of plants that could survive here. But the colonists had introduced small animals and livestock, around where they lived, in the towns that were built a few decades later; then the groups of people were brought in, to occupy the towns. There were a few adults, but mostly the new colonists were children; they had grown up and she and Bertevertree were of generations who had grown up later here on this planet.

The townspeople had been educated, particularly in subjects more applicable to the relatively low-tech life sustainable here at first. They had been taught that in the past, there had been a kind of men who fought with other men so as to hoard the reproducing woman for their mates, and the resulting generations bred a violent and brutal culture, thus it was not permitted for that to happen in any town. But each town was self-governing; and in this town, apparently something like the forbidden polygamist-minded mens's rule had been created, hidden by the phony leaving of any man who was not of the ruling bunch of clever tough men, yet still wanted to find a mate among the town's women. So in their town, the new generation being born even now, would be fathered by the more brutal and cunning men that ruled the town, supposedly honorably. Thus the next generation in their town would have a surplus of the wrong kind of men, for advancing life on this planet.

Anyway, the two of them got the second portable light's battery partially charged up, one cell at a time, by the end of the day.

10   THEIR SPRINGTIME CABIN

Lorimorning was almost relieved to have him ask to take the hand-crank generator with him the next day; she had had much too much familiarity with that generator the past two days as it was. Besides, she seemed to be healing up fine with not so much of the healing currents of that little generator going through her injured arm and leg.

So Burtevertree took the little hand generator with him to the truck the next morning, after their walk in the snow tunnel to strengthen her injured limbs.

Arriving at the truck's big battery, he began the tedious cranking on the hand-generator, a constant number of times, for each cell. It took hours, stopping to rest at times. Once through all the cells, he rummaged around in the pile of electrical stuff he had set around where he had sat the big battery, searching for wire and a light fixture that would work on the battery's voltage. The junk in the back of the truck had higher powered lights; everything in town used the same direct-current 24 volt electrical system, but required higher currents than could draw from this one battery. Finally he decided he had to get interior lights out of the cab of the truck, for use in this test. And they would likely be what would be used for interior lighting of their home, eventually. So he was very careful to preserve the light bulbs, connectors and wiring as he removed them from the truck. He used some of that to make a brief half-second-long touch to the battery, and the light bulb lit up nicely. So for now, the truck battery was halted in its slow march to dysfunction while being fully discharged. That gave him more time for doing other things; but this was enough for one day. He carried one wiring harness and light bulb assembly back with him to home, was all.

On his way back home, however, he paused to climb up packed snow steps to look out a vent hole he had made in the shelter of a tree; it looked like the trees had shed most of the snow, and it was not being replaced by fresh snow. That meant that perhaps spring was soon to follow. And spring thaws meant that things likely would be flooded awhile.

He greeted Lorimorning with that news that evening. She replied that she did not want to drown in here despite it being her comfy home right now. She wanted to be walked to see the cave, tomorrow. They could take one of their partly charged battery powered lights, to make the trip worthwhile; and she would also bring along a basket of seeds and nuts, to store there. They had little to spare, but she wanted a little food stored there, in case they had to make a panic retreat to the cave. Food for two meals seemed not much, but if they found themselves in a world consisting of a huge lake, a couple of meals would be a little comforting, she declared.

They set out early the next morning, he carrying her cane along with the battery powered light and food for the trip; and she carrying the arm sling, but used to hold the little basket of seeds. They went slowly and carefully; and when they stopped to rest midway, after a snack, before they got started, she dug out a branch of a tree protruding a bit into the snow tunnel, broke off a piece, said it was a start for firewood to be stored at their cave home.

By the time they reached the base of the snow steps leading up to the cave, she was really tired. But she had him help her up the steps, while she again said they needed to make a ladder that could be pulled up to prevent access from the ground in summer. Inside the front of the cave, she looked around for awhile, then asked to be helped to see a bit further into the cave, he cranking on the hand flashlight so they could see. They got as far as to see the edge of the underground pond that apparently had an exit that maintained its depth even here, then she was ready to go back to the front of the cave. There they sat down and had their evening meal; it was clear that they were not going to be able to get back home before dark, and he did not have strength to both prop her up and also crank on the flashlight going through the snow tunnel.

He agreed, although not liking the prospect of no fire for warmth, nothing soft and somewhat warm on which to rest. She picked out an area of relative flatness, cleared it of debris, and with a little smile pronounced it their springtime cabin.

It was still daylight, however, so Burtevertree went out to gather whatever he could from the shrubbery near the snow tunnel, starting several minutes walk from their cave; he thought the closer supplies might need to be gathered later in a hurry. The snow had apparently stopped falling many days ago, not having to brush new snow off the truck in recent times there, he realized. He found a tree of a kind that he knew had edibles on it, and dug toward its center, harvesting four out of every five of the tree nuts it had on its branches; also he broke off some of its deadwood branches, and finally scooped up some of the looser fallen leaves under the tree.

Back at the cave, he spread the leaves on the cave floor where Lorimorning had cleaned the cave floor for a sleeping spot, saying they might be softer than the cave floor; and in a few days they would have dried and be a bit of bedding. She thanked him but said they were going back in the morning; their little hearth fire needed tending so as to not go out, for one thing. As it got dark, they did their best to be warm soft comfort for each other, at least a little bit, despite the rocky cold cave floor surface elsewhere. And before she fell asleep, she said yes, the leaves were indeed nicer for her head on which to rest.

But in the morning, she was not in the mood for a long walk. Still stiff from the extra exercise yesterday, and sore in places from the hard bedding in the night, she said she was not eager for the journey home, despite its comforts awaiting. Perhaps he could return home and bring food for a couple more meals, along with a bit of their dry leaf bedding; replenish the hearth's fire supplies, and then return to the cave. If he got back in time and she felt better, they could head home in the afternoon; but if not, they would have a little more comfort for another night's stay here. And she pointed out that they really needed to do a lot to make this cave area habitable, and all the supplies and provisions that they could bring here, would increase their chances for surviving in the cave, if the area below flooded. Even a big bag of dry leaves from their underground home's diggings, would provide cushioning, insulation, and even fuel for a small fire later. She said to use one of the pieces of spare clothing they had removed from the remains of the assaulters, and fill it with dry leaves and include twigs for starting a small fire here in the cave.

When he returned that evening with the supplies she had requested, he found that she had managed to use the snow packed steps to go down, and had gathered a few flat pieces of rock at the base of the cliff, and had used them to make a little hearth near the front of the cave, but not where it would be visible from outside the cave, although smoke would still be visible. A small hearth-fire would not make much smoke, yet it could keep a bit of fire going for larger warmth and cooking fires at night when smoke would not be visible. But for tonight, no fire; but the bundle of dry leaves made their second night in this second home, a lot more comfortable than their first sleep here.

In the morning, she insisted that they get started home without breakfast. They still had enough food here for a couple meals, but she preferred to save them for emergencies; and so they tidied up their space here, went down the snow steps, and began the slow walk home. This time they stopped often, despite her protests that she was fine. They gathered a few frozen fruit at one resting place, however; thawed out when home, it would make a fine meal. She was still strong enough to get herself down into their underground home with only a little help from him; and soon she had some soup cooking in her stone bowl, a welcome treat for them before a nice snuggle in warm softness tonight.

11   SPRING SURPRISES

Burtevertree resumed his daily scavenging for parts from the truck and for edibles and tree deadwood, bringing some to each of their homes. He even brought seats from the truck to the cave home; he remembering too well the nights he had spent on that hard cave floor, leaves cushioning or not. He took all of the wiring and possibly useful electrical parts to the cave, to protect them from the expected flooding. He used the second of the two hand trucks to haul the heavy battery to the base of the cliff, but the snow steps would not support his weight and the battery weight too, so for now he left it at the base of the cliff near the cave entrance. He got the small external combustion starter-idler engine loose from the truck's engine compartment and got it up into the cave.

Meanwhile, Lorimorning had been exercising herself with short walks alone, staying near home. She even had been able to gather some more edibles and firewood along the way. They discussed the impending potential flood in the evenings and mornings before he headed out to work; and she provided him with parcels to take to the cave each morning. She was being careful to make sure that there remained supplies here too; the collapse of the snow tunnels might block them here before they could get to the cave. She even made a small hearth fire to take over to the cave, for him to tend each day, a small source of fire to help survival in the cave if they had to scramble to get there.

One evening as he was heading back home, he heard a dull boom in the distance. He thought it came from down the snow tunnel that went to the truck. Then another boom, louder. He suspected it was the arch falling in the snow tunnel somewhere. But it was suddenly getting louder from both directions, he could feel the shaking of the tunnel's walls; he ran for the underground home.

He woke up, partly buried in the snow; the arch had fallen in and had stunned him. It was still daylight, so he could not have been unconscious very long, he thought. Sitting up in the snow, he could easily see the trench leading in both directions, but he was not sure which direction was to their home. He dug out the supplies that he had been carrying, and set them to the side of the trench, arranging them to point like an arrow, in the direction he had decided to take at first. Apparently the whole snow tunnel had collapsed together everywhere; the snow was fairly well packed on the floor of the trench.

He remembered having passed the intersection where the tunnel to the truck had been; it could not be far away, if he was walking in the wrong direction. Surely he would be able to see the intersection of the trenches. But no such intersection was found after an hour's walking; and then he came to the end of the trench. He started digging down at the end of the trench with his hands, having no scoop. But he did not find the door to his home. Then he discovered twigs and leaves mixed in his diggings; he realized that apparently the collapse of the snow arch in front of his doorway might have collapsed his roof of little branches and twigs, leaf covered, intended only for a light covering of show. He dug down through the mix of twigs and snow, found what had been the floor of his upper room, Then he dug toward the ramp to their lower room; the area over there had not collapsed, He heard Lorimorning calling from below, before he broke through.

She had heard and felt the rumble of the tunnel collapsing, and had hurried down into the deeper stronger part of their home, and had just gotten in there when the roof caved in on their upper room. There was no air inlet anymore for the lower hearth, so she had to extinguish it, lest it use up the oxygen in there.

Well, the situation seemed to have reached a stable state for now,

They had an air inlet through the ramp to the remains of their upper room, but they had no fire remaining on the hearth.

If the snow archway had collapsed, that meant they were softening from melt. It would probably not be safe to stay down here, if flooding indeed did happen. The next morning, they gathered up what clothing and supplies they could find, spending a lot of time digging for the hand crank flashlight. They lifted all the good stuff up out of the lower room, to pile on the floor of the collapsed snow tunnel, there by their former upper room's remains; then they started trudging down the trench, dragging one of the jackets stuffed with supplies. Lorimorning made sure she had the hand crank generator among the few things she carried in her former arm sling. She stepped into the snow depressions left by Burtevertree, as he slowly made his way down the trench. They passed by his little arrow on the side of the trench; he could come get the items another day, he hoped. It became dusk, and it became harder to identify the sides of the trench, and for her to find his snow depressions. Finally it was too dark, and she spun the handle on the little flashlight just enough so they could memorize the looks of the trench ahead, and then they would make more progress down the trench.

Finally they bumped into the snow steps up to the cave, and he helped her up the steps and into the cave. By the time he had hauled their bundle being dragged along, up into the cave, she had the hearth fire going nicely; she warmed some soup in the stone bowl she had brought along, there by the little fire. And they slept well on the cushions from the truck seats that night.

They had made the move to their springtime home. Not as easily or well-managed as they had hoped; but it was nice to have an alternate living space somewhat prepared.

Looking out the cave's entrance the next day, Burtevertree commented that the area was looking unchanged, except for the entrance leading away from the steps leading up here. Lorimorning looked out there too, and after a moment replied that it looked like the same place that had collapsed, and still was in the unstable mode waiting for excuse to collapse some more. He pointed out that the big battery was still down below needing bringing up here before flood, but she pointed out that they still did not have a ladder made that would reach up here from the ground. The snow packed steps by which they climbed up here, were not likely to support the weight of Burtevertree and the battery together, yet finding any materials for building a ladder to support such a weight was even less likely.

Finally he agreed to skip going back to their former home to bring more of their belongings over here, but instead to go find the nearest branches strong enough and long enough for a ladder up here, plus at least a few smaller branches for a few rungs for the ladder; and while doing that, lift the heavy battery up to the first step on the compressed snow steps coming up here. Then look for branches for ladder, If the battery was still there when he came back, he would lift the battery up to the next step, and place it there. There were nine steps that he had made long ago to gain access to the cave, and he had added compressed snow to the same steps since then; they were almost like ice in their strength. By the time he had done the routine, he had the two long branches for the ladder and two rung-sized branches put up into the front of the cave, and the huge battery was on the sixth of the compressed snow steps. And the sun was getting higher in the sky, it was only getting warmer. He broke the routine, and lifted the battery up to the seventh step, eighth, ninth and it was on the stone ledge in front of the cave.

Lorimorning busied herself with cutting notches for the lowest and highest rungs of the ladder, and using strands of the unwound rope they had saved, while he went searching for more branches appropriate to the other rungs of the ladder. Bringing the branches up the snow steps, he was almost expecting them to collapse under him, but they stayed firm; he was back in their cave home, the ladder was on its way for being completed, and he was ready for dinner.

Resting after dinner, watching the little fire warming them, Lorimorning thanked him for his great work in making this and their former home come into existence. She said she intended to do her best to make this a new home for them. And more, she intended to bring forth many children by him in the future they had together.

She was quiet a long time, then said that she was remembering back when she and her girlfriend hitchhiked aboard the truck, curious as to what was happening to her friend's boyfriend. Then when they saw the two men throwing the boyfriend over the cliff, the two women ran and attempted to prevent that from happening, but it unbalanced all five of them and as they went over the cliff, Lorimorning saw the face of one of the abductors. She had barely time to feel the shock as they went over the cliff together.

She was quiet a long time again, and Burtevertree was almost falling asleep. She resumed her monologue to him. The face of the man she saw as they went over the cliff, was perhaps the same man who was of the town leaders, who most often had been visiting her as a mate for several months previously; she had agreed to that happening, when it was clear that Burtevertree had rejected her and had left to go to the distant town where there was more opportunity and better women, she was told. She was now already with child by the town leader. They were going to have a child to take care of in a few months, and it was not Burtevertree's. Nonetheless it would be her child, and future ones would be by Burtevertree. Just like the snow tunnel collapsing and all the complications about that, life seemed to always have the complications to her; yet, all the events of life needed to be navigated and resolved, she said.

Burtevertree was more awake now, realizing what she had just said. Actually, she had said a lot in a few phrases. Life had been complicated too for him, and still was complicated.

But as they snuggled together comfortably that night, finally in real comfort on the cushions from the truck and covered by multiple layers of clothing, and the little fire glowing softly to the side, life did not feel all that bad to him.

12 FARM ANIMALS

When all the rungs were tied into the notches on the two long branches, they practiced climbing up and down the ladder, laying it over the top of the compressed snow steps. The scene out across the sunken area surrounded by the high cliffs, seemed to not change; there was still much that could be salvaged from both the truck and their former home. But Lorimorning said no, it was not worth the risks. He thought he could make at least one trip to each of these places and bring back more things to help their survival chances; she said no, he might not be able to make it back if he did so; remember when he was out there and the arches over the tunnel started to collapse? She thought it was like that out there, right now.

It looked the same as it did before, to him. After a couple of days of being idle in the cave, he decided to at least go gather nearby things from the trees. She anxiously watched him as he stepped onto the first snow step; then the step turned to mush under his foot, and he was down in a pile of slush at the foot of the ladder. The undisturbed snow loomed several feet above him as he lay for a moment at the base of the cliff; then he quickly climbed up the ladder, pulling it up after him.

The next morning, they both looked out at what appeared to be a vast uniform slush pond. Somewhere out there was the pieces of the truck. Somewhere even further out there was the lower room of their former room, no doubt filled with ice slush now. Spring was on its way, and was going to have its way with the landscape.

They took the hand crank flashlight to light up their way, as they explored the back cave tunnel. They went past the pool of water that had the little stream from further up the cave, ever flowing into the pool but it never rising higher. They walked alongside the little stream; she commented that unlike the part of the cave in which they now lived, this tunnel was scoured clean; it probably had much higher rates of water flowing down it at times. And it could be that springtime melt was when that would happen. They did not want to be anywhere along here when the water started pouring down here. But there seemed to be no more water than usual at this point, and eventually they reached the area where he had discovered an access hole was in sight of the truck. The snow pack around the cave's entrance seemed to be slumping like the rest of the snow. They hurried back down the tunnel, back past the pond, to their hopefully safe and dry living place.

They had lost one of their bundles of supplies, the one they had left behind on their hurried trip here through the trenches, dragging the other bundle. That one had their saved food, mostly. Thus it was probably the most important bundle to have brought here. Getting more edibles from the snow such that now covered the land, was probably not possible. The cloudy weather did not seem to be urging the vast lake out there to subside that they could tell.

They went into the minimum food and fire wood consumption mode. They did not need so much food anyway, not doing the heavy work as had been done before. The hard part was the idleness in the cave, with little to do. She made little strips from the leather jacket they had used for toting supplies here; the strips of leather she cut off, were used to more securely tie the rungs of the ladder.

He busied himself by arranging the materials scavenged from the truck, sorting into piles of similar things. Pieces of wire in one pile. The light bulbs and light sockets in the next pile. Switches and connectors in another pile. The huge battery by itself, then the little external combustion engine sitting at an awkward angle next to the battery. He spent a day using their hand crank generator to charge up each of the cells in the huge battery, more to preserve the battery than to save any useful energy.

The days went by and finally Lorimorning pointed out that she could see lots more of the trees, out there in the ice slush world below them. He cautiously set the ladder down to solid surface outside their cave, pulled it back up again; there was only about ankle-deep water out there now. They began to plan what next.

Tree fruit would be inedible by now. Seeds and nuts would be falling off branches into the ground below. They needed to gather as much of the seeds and nuts as possible, while also continuing to leave ten percent of all seeds and nuts where they were, to let the plants renew themselves. but how soon could they dare go walk out there? They had no boots; ice slushy stirring would quickly deplete them of body warmth. They would have to wait until they were able to walk out there without sinking in.

Then the sound of lots of water was heard from deep in the back cave; its loudness started to fade after a couple of days, so they again made a trip down the back tunnel to the little pond. Water indeed was filling the further tunnel side to side, but only a few inches deep; and indeed the pond did not look any higher than before. They seemed safe from inundation, in their little up-front cave home. Burtevertree had become curious about the cave's passage that went beyond the egress hole up on top of the cliff near the road where the truck had been; but he was going to have to wait until the flow rate of water was less than now, to go exploring again.

Lorimorning spent a lot of time chipping stone against stone, enlarging the natural crevices in the cave walls, and eventually shelf space was apparently being made. She pointed out that when they were back here a year from now, they would have a little one to care for, and this place needed to be made lots more functional. Besides, banging away at the rocks helped keep her strength up, and was a little bit of artistic expression, reminding her that she was not entirely ruled by the whims of nature. Once he saw the plan for shelving along the cave walls, he too picked up a rock and began the slow process of chipping away rock so as to make shelf space appear in the cave wall. In fact, he would like to get some of the piles of truck pieces and electrical junk pieces up off the cave floor, to have more living room.

He also began to realize that not only the cave wall was changing shape by the banging of loose rocks on the wall; that the rocks he used to chip away at the cave wall were also getting reshaped in the same process. He then started choosing loose rocks used for chipping on the wall, so as to end up with shaped loose rocks intended to become the base for the irregular-shaped external combustion engine's support. He then began to build that base and soon had enough of a stone base made to place the little engine there, up near enough to the front of the cave so as to provide escape of its exhaust smoke. Perhaps eventually he could scavenge tailpipe from the remains of the truck, and make a stovepipe for the little engine, but it would be a long time before that could happen.

She too had begun to combine the shaping of building blocks along with making cave wall shelving. Stone blocks were getting made, and in time it appeared to be base blocks for some large flat rock as yet unfound, to make a little table.

Reflecting one evening at the evident total lack of small animals in the sunken cliff-ringed valley that was their home range now, Lorimorning said that they ought to be able to go use her bow and arrows to hunt small game on top of the cliff, especially far from the road. So when the water coming down the cave tunnel into the pond had reduced to where there was dry path all the way to the access hole, they went hunting up on top of the cliff. She asked him to be patient and learn by watching how she used the bow and arrows; she only had made three arrows, and it was too easy to lose an arrow in the vegetation. So his practice would have to wait. Yet still he was able to gather firewood along the way, and even a few green branches that she said looked promising for making more arrows.

He was not trained to be a hunter, but she had learned to be one from an early age, as a food provider for her family. He could not see any animals, but eventually having lost only one of her arrows, she had gotten a large rodent animal. There was a shallow burrow there, and she had dispatched several little young ones before Burtevertree asked to save a few of them; perhaps they could be raised down below, starting a little farm with them, and not have to go up here hunting all the time. Made sense to her, so they kept the last five of the little animals alive. Burtevertree was going to have to look after them, however.

Well, in the cave, he soon found that keeping track of the little creatures was not so easy. They seemed to like running all over the place, and already a couple of them had managed to fall off the edge of the cave down into the area below the cliff; he could not see them down there, so he assumed that they had survived and were off foraging in the mushy ground out there. It looked like eventually Lorimorning would be able to go hunting down here too, if the little animals survived and thrived down there.

Their next hunting trip was not only for more stew meat, but this time was to gather all the little ones for transplanting to their farm and valley floor. This clearly was the season for gathering the little ones, just at the age where they were weaned and learning to forage for themselves. They seemed to fear nothing, so apparently there were no natural enemies, other than people. And the hunters began to use the same principle as with the seeds and nuts, to leave some of the creatures alone with their nests, so as to be able to re-populate the area more easily for next year.

13 TOWN LIGHTS

The ground surface of the sunken valley had become firm enough for them to walk on easily again, so they resumed their seeking edibles from among the vegetation down there as before, only ranging in different areas than before. Eventually they found their former below-ground home's remains; the upper section had been crushed in before they left, and besides, it and the lower floor were still filled with water. They pulled away the former roofing materials, and as the water continued to subside, they began to prepare to rebuild it. The site was fairly well hidden by the trees, so they discussed how to build it so it would have an upper floor that would survive the flood stage, now that they knew how deep that water would be. Maybe it would be too cold to stay there all winter and spring, and would certainly be in isolation unless they made a canoe, but an alternate living area seemed wise for them to create. If nothing else, it could be used to store some stuff kept dry through spring, over here.

Burtevertree began to realize that since the floor of the sunken valley became covered with water in spring, unlike the plateau surrounding the valley, that the little creatures could not survive the flood stage. So he also made plans for making a raised shelter area for the little animals to make a few burrows, hopefully stocking them with seeds and nuts from the area, before winter set in, just like they did in the surrounding area. It was looking like a lot of work to be done

They now had their choice of firewood and structural wood, from both down in the valley, and from the vast area above the valley.

They had the two knives salvaged from the truck's stuff, but there was only so much that could be done by whittling. Without a saw, branches over five cm thick were impractical to gather. They made a trip over to the remains of the truck; it was a lot more rusty, and covered with a layer of dirt, but they were able to find a couple o saw blades; their handles had been broken, and had been tossed in the back of the truck as junk. One was a fine-toothed hacksaw; the other was a carpenter's saw blade.

They both worked on the project of making handles for the two saws. He was able to uncomfortably use the raw frame of the hacksaw to rough shape handles for both kinds of saw, then she used stone shards as sandpaper to shape the hacksaw handle. Then he was able to use the hacksaw to speed up the shaping of the carpenter's saw's new handle. And once the carpenter's saw was back useable, they were able to cut tree branches 10 cm or 15 cm in diameter, much better for building some kinds of things. They would be needed to make strong poles for the support of the raised floor level of their rebuild of the winter home, for one thing. And then a stronger ladder for getting up and down to the cave entrance, too.

On their next hunting trip on top of the plateau, she made special effort to teach him archery. She had been taught from childhood and it seemed natural to her; but it seemed that he was very poor at both shooting an arrow where he wanted it to go, as well as poor at spotting little animals in the brush. But she told him that he was going to have to do it; she was getting heavy with child and would not always be able to go on the hunt with him, at least for a month or so.

They made a side trip over to the original site of the roadside place where the truck had been parked, and from where both of them had been dropped over the side. There did not seem to have been any vehicles come here since, nor even have used the dirt road in a long time. Lorimorning pointed out an odd-looking pile of brush not far away; going over to it, hidden in the brush they found lots of shoes, boots, belts, carrying cases; apparently removed from the townsmen's victims before tossing them over the side of the cliff.

She said it looked like a new resource for them, but he said it was like grave robbers. She said it was more like robbing the grave robbers; and anyway they had been using things that had been worn by the two men who had been disposing of the non-celibate men of the town. Here was lots of leather, some ruined by years of weather. Some maybe with useful material. The carrying bags looked useful and apparently had not been emptied, so whatever personal belongings the victims had with them when they were abducted, were probably still in the bags. So they gathered up as many of the carrying bags as they could carry, and took them down into their cave home, sorted through the potentially useful items that were in the bags, and hung the bags up to dry. For now, they had no urge to go back for more. It was just too sad remembering the men friends who had suddenly "left town to go find opportunity elsewhere" as told by the Tealer town leaders, so many times over the years. They had seen hundreds of pairs of shoes and boots; it surely was the count of those who had been abducted and disposed of over the side here.

The question was, would there some day be another truck come here, and toss off someone else, taking over the task of the two missing abductors? Lorimorning said the town would still be having its young men gain adulthood and start ignoring the claim by the town's leaders that the non-Tealer men must remain celibate, so how was the town dealing with that, she wondered. Burtevertree remembered his experiences, of longing to meet and be with Lorimorning, and feelings that celibacy was not the best thing to happen. Then he had been abducted. Lorimorning filled in that she too had wanted to be with him. The men of the town leadership tended to be a bit brutal, and besides, each had many women besides her. It was a life neither of them wanted to return to. There would be no tolerance for the two of them to live together and be mates in the town.

Yet life out here was rough. They had survived so far, but how long could just the two of them cope with everything that nature gave them? They had been through one full season cycle, and knew a lot about all that. They now had access to both above and below the cliffs.

One place they had yet to explore was the rest of the cave beyond where it had an access hole up here. She was getting heavy and hunting was just not her thing anymore. So they decided to explore a ways into the cave, while she still could walk a long ways.

They took turns cranking on the handle of the generator-flashlight; both had built up endurance to some extent for cranking on that handle. As in the prior part of the tunnel, there was the little stream of water flowing down it; they still did not know the source of the water that filled their cave pool. There was a gentle upslope of the cave floor, apparently matching the similar upslope of the terrain above; then the tunnel was suddenly filled with dirt and brush. An entrance to the world must lie just beyond, what was out there? Burtevertree broke through the branches along one side of the cave tunnel, breaking through to find a somewhat depressed area of the land, with a large lake in it; and this was the edge of the lake.

It was getting to be dusk; no matter, it would be dark in the cave tunnel as they went back home, cranking on the flashlight. So they stayed out there for awhile, enjoying the fresh air, the sounds of life stirring around the edge of the little lake, savoring the moment.

Then they saw a light come on, over on the far edge of the lake. then another light. Soon it was apparent that the other edge of the lake was where a town had been built. Not their town; they knew of no lake anywhere nearby where they had grown up. Would the people there be hostile toward them? Their town's leaders had said all towns were far apart, and generally had strict laws against migration among them. There was a story about a couple, a man and a woman, who had come to their town; the townsmen had killed the man, but the woman begged for mercy and so she had been accepted into the breeding stock of their town. The town's leaders said there was only one town, far away, that accepted men, and that was where the young men had chosen to go, when they decided they no longer would accept celibacy here. Would the town over there at the far side of this lake be the same way? Or would they welcome strangers to be among them? Now was not the time to be exploring that option, they agreed; they pulled a bit of brush in to seal the exit hole they had made from the cave, and began the long hand-cranking journey down the cave tunnel. Past the upper exit hole and eventually back to their cave entrance springtime abode; then asleep at last, after a cold meal of seeds and nuts.

14 EXPLORING ALONG THE CLIFF

Morning came; Lorimorning heated up some tea in her little stone bowl, from which they both drank until it was empty. Then she heated up a soup of mashed seeds and nuts for breakfast, with some dried meat from the hunts in the past. They rested there a couple days; Burtevertree finally got the external combustion engine running. He still needed to connect the truck's generator to the little engine, and then they would have lots of electrical energy to finally recharge the big battery from the truck.

Although he would rather have made a frame for the motor generator out of metal, it was quicker to make the frame out of wood from tree branches, notched and tied together. It seemed configured enough to keep the external combustion chamber from setting the framework on fire; and if it did, he thought if the frame burned up it would not destroy the engine nor generator.

Finally he put water and kindling into the little steam engine, got it running again, this time with it driving the generator. It's output voltage looked adequate, so he connected it to the voltage regulator, and its output looked like it would be fine to not overcharge a battery. Then he let the engine stop from lack of more firewood, and he wrapped some of the more sturdy wires around the battery posts, connecting to the voltage regulator and it to the generator's output. The voltage regulator also prevented the battery's voltage from passing back to the generator when the generator was not running, he verified. Then starting up the little steam engine, he soon verified the voltage across the big battery was slowly rising. He had to keep watch over the fuel supply to the steam engine, but that was a lot easier than cranking on the little flashlight generator to put a little energy into each cell individually to the big truck battery as he had been doing to keep the battery from self-discharging to ruin. It took several hours before the voltage regulator dropped out, indicating that adding more energy to the battery would begin to cause outgassing and start to damage the battery a little, so he shut the steam engine down, finally done with that task. Hooking a small light through a switch to the battery, he briefly verified that it produced light.

Meantime, they were both thinking about the implications of what appeared to be a human settlement, close to a lake at the far end of this tunnel. Burtevertree thought that it would be difficult for those people to reach the cave, it being at the far edge of the lake, and the mouth of the cave was hidden by underbrush. There appeared to be some kind of outcropping at the cave mouth; the impression was it had been a fairly vertical face, not easy to climb down to gain access. A floating object, a boat or raft, would be needed to reach the cave from the town. But Lorimorning pointed out that some people knew how to swim and perhaps when it was warmer could even swim over to where the mouth of the cave was. It seemed that there was risk of discovering invaders suddenly appearing right here at their spring home. And in general people do not welcome outsiders into town.

Perhaps the tunnel could be sealed off, making it look like it stopped, such as where the access hole to the plateau above them was. They could fill in the side of the tunnel that contained their passageway to here, maybe leaving a small hole for providing a bit of air flow. But then they could not gain access to the plateau, and they needed to do hunting up there, both for meat for meals, but also for nests of small animals that could be taken down here into their farm areas to raise as livestock. Access to the plateau was also needed for gathering of deadwood for heat and cooking; select branches were also available up there without disturbing their own sunken valley ecosystem. They could fill up the tunnel as it came from the lakeside entrance, but any explorers of the cave might be tempted to dig away what looked like a rockfall, to see what was on the other side. And the whole cave might be well known to the townspeople, not likely it would have remained unknown so near to town. Coming to no decision, they agreed to make more visits to the far end of the tunnel and see what else they could learn about the situation over there.

They also thought it would be wise to see if the sunken valley where they now had made their home, had any of the more distant parts that had survived the spring thaw without being flooded. Gathering up supplies for a day's trip, they set off on a long hike, staying close to the cliff wall that surrounded the sunken valley. They then could always find their way back home, by following the cliff wall, if they lost their orientation. It was too easy to lose sight of anything familiar including the cliff wall, out there in the dense tree and underbrush area. They chose the direction along the cliff face that led away from the site where the truck and the many remains still needing burying, where the abductors had been tossing their victims over the decades. Right now they were not interested in renewing knowledge of that place, even though it was where they had begun this adventure together.

They set out on their hike right after breakfast the next day, planning on starting their return a bit before midday, so as to be back home before dark. They were not well equipped to spend the night in the open; they did have enough food for a second day, however. It was slow going, sometimes finding the edge of the pile of stone shards along the base of the cliff was easiest, other times it was easier to progress under the trees a ways, but making sure they could find the face of the cliff soon after making that kind of pathway.

They eventually decided it was time to reverse their direction and head home, so they cleared off a little area at the base of the cliff, and set out their little picnic. It was a time to relax and chat; nearly all their conversation up until now was just to facilitate their seemingly endless survival challenges up to this point.

The boys and girls had been kept separate in the town, and as young adults they only encountered each other as part of work duties; and friendliness, even idle conversation between men and women, was forbidden. Only the group of Tealer men who were the town leaders, were allowed to visit the women. So they really had a lot to share with each other, to learn about each other's ways.

Lorimorning said she was very glad to have her own man as constant companion; she had longed for that to be, even in her teens; when she became old enough, then one or the other of the Tealer town's leaders would visit her at night. She did not definitely know which one of them was the father of the child she was carrying. She was already looking forward to Burtevertree helping raise her child and to then have children by him after that, children who she know who their father was. They talked about the stories they were taught as they grew up; most stories related to work tasks they would do when they were adults; the women more learning about raising children, homemaking, cooking, and making clothes. Men were more into building homes, streets, machinery, expanding the living space and utility of the town. The town's leaders were the main teachers of both men and women, and usually each lesson was immediately followed by a work assignment that applied what had been learned that day.

There were also the history lessons, which were taught only rarely, usually to reinforce the instruction that the small group of thirty Tealer men who were the town's leaders, were the only special men who were to be followed and obeyed. But there was the history about the colonizing of this planet, how there had been seed ships that flew everywhere, spreading seeds, the starts for the life now thriving all around here. The first seedships delivered mostly microbiota, lichens, cyanobacteria. Loose metals were bound up by some of those tiny creatures, and other creatures made the soil such that small plants could then grow. Leaves would fall in winter, and a layer to the rocky land was formed by the disintegrating leaves and twigs. It had been about a hundred years until the seedships began placing small groups of people around the planet, along with small herbivore animals, which were partially kept confined on the human camps, but eventually some animals escaped, and now years later the hunting could be done in the woods.

Lorimorning had been taught how to hunt for the little animals in the forest, bringing them back to provide special meat treats for a meal or two, as they were animals not controlled by the settlement's farms. She had shown special skill in archery and of the hunt, and thus was especially welcomed to go out to do hunting.

Burtevertree was chatting about the seedships and what he had been taught about the history of the seedships, where was their base of operations; she thought that the seedships had been removed from the planet for use elsewhere, once their job had been competed. She did say that many of the seedships had gotten damaged or parts wore out and they failed.

Lorimorning seemed drawn into that thought train, not one she had much explored before. But it was interesting now. Burtevertree noticed that when she talked about the seedships and about their losses, she looked a lot in one direction. Finally he asked her did she see an animal hiding in the brush over there, what were her trained hunter's eyes drawn to, over there. She said she was not aware of an interest in that particular place, but now that he mentioned it, she thought something looked different about the area; it was right at the edge of the little clearing at the base of the cliff where they were picnicking now. She declared that in fact it seemed strange that so large an area did not have any trees growing on it; there must be a shelf to the cliff face, under these leaves. Using their walking sticks to dig away the top leaves, down only a few inches was a hard flat surface. But, it was not rock there. Odd.

Moments later they had found that under them was a huge gently curving smooth surface. Over right next to the cliff face, the smooth surface suddenly showed jagged edges; was this one of the crashed seedships of ancient times?

By that time that they had figured out that the large object was made of a material that did not bend on impact, but had just broken off pieces.

They had no interest now in making the hike back home; they would not reach there before dark anyway, due to their time digging here. Their hand-crank flashlight would probably not have ensured they could find the cliff face again in the path that went through the trees and underbrush in places. So they decided they were going to spend the night here. And so they busied themselves digging along the edge between the cliff face and the fractured edge of the large smooth surface object; and by dusk, they had dug access to be under the edge of the mysterious thing, and had made a little cave for themselves that way. They used the flashlight to peer around; there seemed to be a large empty area off away from the broken edge here. But for now they had a cave-like shelter, a bit warmer in here. They made themselves a bedded area, and slept soundly.

15 CRASHED SEEDSHIP

The sun had risen quite a ways by the time the light had reached them and got them awake. Lorimorning prepared them a breakfast of seed cake and nuts, with some strips of dried meat. But they had no makings for a fire or heating a refreshing liquid.

They cleared out more debris in the interface between cliff and broken shell's edge, letting more light in. They clambered down the slope of debris, then reached the groundwater level. It seemed to be a huge gently curving shell structure, all empty as far as they could see, although that was not far with their little flashlight with only a little help from sunshine filtering in. They dug around with their walking sticks, looking for pieces of broken material, but found none. Finally on the far edge of the accessible volume, they found a round hole about a meter in diameter in the shell structure; looking in the debris near there, indeed they found what must have been the cover plate of the hole. It formed a shallow bowl of about a meter in diameter; the material was unmarred, and was much lighter than equivalent rock solid material. Climbing out of the place, Lorimorning tied the round object onto Burtevertree's backpack, while she would carry all their hiking materials they had brought along. Then they headed back toward home.

Midday they arrived back in their cave-front home, and soon were treated with the shared stone bowl of heated broth made by Lorimorning, a time to relax. All seemed the same as before in their world. Except for the meter-diameter shallow curved circular plate thing they had brought back, reminding them that there was a larger world out there. And then they remembered the other end of their cave tunnel, from where could be seen a town of strangers, representing either a danger or an opportunity for their future.

Lorimorning said that after she had given birth and Bertevertree could adequately care for the child for awhile, she could possibly go make contact with the people of the town. A woman in her fertile years was more likely to be accepted into a town of strangers, than a potentially rival man would be.

But Burtevertree was more interested in further exploring the crash site of what apparently had been an ancient seed ship that had helped bring the diversity of life to this planet long ago. He was wanting to learn first hand about history, which he was beginning to suspect was a bit warped by the small group of Tealer men who also were the teachers and rule-makers of the town. The boys and girls of the town being kept separated in schooling and as they were becoming adult, the men were separated to go live with the men of the town, and the young women went to live with the women of the town. The group of thirty Tealer men who were the town leaders, were the only men allowed to be intimate with the women who were in their fertile years; middle-aged women then were sent over to partner with the single men of the town, keeping them company and cooking for them, sewing their clothes and living in the houses the men had built.

The Tealers taught that this separation of men and women had always been that way throughout time, and had been decreed the law even in the time of the seedships who had planted this world with diverse micro life forms and plants. Then other seedships came, and set up the scattered towns around the planet.

The two compared notes on the teachings by the town leaders, and that part seemed the same. But other parts of what was taught was different, they discovered. And it was not just that the women were taught to provide the food and clothing, and the single-men were taught to build and maintain the buildings and streets of the town. Lorimorning pointed out that if it were not for the many men who had been abducted by the town's leaders and disposed of over the cliff, there would have been about the same number of men as there were women, so did that not mean that the creators meant for men and women to pair up and live life together? Burtevertree thought about it and agreed, that seemed reasonable, and would be a nicer way of life, he thought. But the group of town leader Tealer men taught that only they were allowed intimacy with the fertile women of the town, and said it was a basic law of the creator of mankind that it be so. She then said it might be interesting to see how the other town out there lived, across the lake, were men and women separated there too?

He began to think that she was getting too interested in the other men of the mystery town at the far end of the tunnel. Maybe it was the influence of her unborn child, that had been fathered by the Tealers, before the fate that had brought them together here. Still, she was being a wonderful companion for him now; and soon she would be quite dependent on him for survival in her giving birth and early months afterwards. But then, would she start wanting to go explore other men again, he thought to himself.

As if sensing his worry, Lorimorning pointed out that she was his mate and would remain so in the future; she had wanted that even before he had supposedly decided to go to some far-away town, as she was told by the town leader men, before they took her as another of their mates for breeding. Now fate had brought them together again, and she was not going to let them part so easily in the future. But she also was a woman of many interests and abilities, and needed lots of companionship of other kinds, too. But only he would be her mate in the future, she also declared.

She also was getting a bit slower in traveling, due to her increasing size. She said they needed to make a planned visit to the crash site, make an extended stay there of a couple of days, then return here to stay until she gave birth. They would need to learn all they could about the seed ship and its history, in that extended stay over there. She began to gather food and supplies for their journey and stay over there, while he collected digging tools, and a small carrying container for a fire start.

As they made their way to the crash site a couple of days later, Burtevertree cleared a better trail, now knowing what was up ahead. Besides, this made it a bit easier going for Lorimorning. Arriving at the opening down into the interior of the crashed seedship, he first dug easy steps down into the hole, while she set her supplies aside and scavenged for shards of stone from the cliff face with which to make a fire hearth, and gathered some twigs for a fire. Then down into the chamber, they assembled the fire hearth and used the fire start that they had brought along, to start a cooking fire, warming them up a bit too. She soon was sharing some warm broth, sipped from her stone bowl.

This time, they carried a fire torch to light up the interior, as they re-explored down to the edge of the water-filled volume of the huge shell structure. It appeared that the only area which had been filled with dirt was that which had flowed in through the hole next to the cliff face, along with a little which had come through the round hole from where their cover plate had come, which was at the water line. He thought it was likely that the only way that water could leave this interior was through that hole, unless there were damage down below. That the current water line was right at the edge of the round hole, suggested that was the situation. This also meant that to get access to the rest of the interior, he would have to remove the water himself. Lorimorning offered her most tight-woven basket that she had used to bring supplies over here; carefully placing the seeds and strips of meat onto the flat stone shards she had gathered above, they then took turns with the basket, dipping water and emptying it out through the round hole in the side of the ship. The basket was not water tight at first, but soon the fibers swelled a bit and very little water was lost between dipping the water and discarding it out the hole.

Burtevertree went outside and while she continued the bailing out of water, he was able to find the area in the underbrush where the water was being tossed, and he dug out the brush, gathering most of it for the fire, but with intent to clear a path for daylight to reach the round hole a lot better. Back inside and taking his turn at bailing water again, it indeed was lots easier to see in here. And, they could see that shapes were being exposed by the lowering of the water, including some that were nearby. However, the shapes appeared to be mounds of moss; yet it was likely that the moss covered something of interest. As soon as they got the water level down far enough that the moss could be scraped off by a stick, they took the moss outside to dry for fire-making later.

By midday the next day, they had the water level down to where they had been able to scrape off moss for less slippery walking, over to the nearer object that they were uncovering from ages of moss growth. It appeared to be a slide rack, and numerous identical objects seemed to still be attached to the rack. Finding the near end of the rack, they slid the end object off, rinsed it off in the water, and took it up to view better. Outside in the bright sunlight, the object seemed to be a carrying container made of two shell sections and a hinge pin. It was not too hard to remove the hinge pin, and the object opened up, exposing a stinky decomposed mess; probably it was a canister of seeds that had never gotten deployed by the seed ship. He took the three pieces back down to the water, cleaned them off best he could, brought them back up into the sunlight for her to examine too.

16 CANISTERS AND BOATS

The object appeared to be a roundish container, with a lid and hinge pin, and a latch on the opposite side to the hinge pin. With the hinge pin removed, it opened up, the lid was easily removed; so the deployment of such containers must have involved sliding off the rack, punching out the hinge pin and dumping the container's contents over the side. Then the container would be pulled further along, the lid shut and back onto the rack, empty now. The material of the container seemed to be the same as the 1-meter diameter curved plate they had retrieved on their first trip here, except this was much thinner. A material much lighter than stone, smoother and yet not exactly metal either. Lorimorning was quick to take the hinge pin over to their fire, and heat up the pin to see if it melted; there was no sign of damage to the pin, so she similarly heated up the lid. It too got cooking-hot without apparent damage.

They collected half a dozen of the canisters, setting them by the opening to the outside; they could not carry them all back home, but this would enable their future retrieval even if water had again filled the chamber below. They planned to carry three of them home on this trip anyway, which would probably be their last one here for a long time.

A complex set of mechanisms appeared as they continued to empty water out; they cleaned the structures off with sticks and water rinse, but what they were for, they could not guess yet. They built a small fire hearth down by the new water edge, got a fire going, verified there was good convection pulling the air through the round hole and then up to exit out the upper access point; it got smoky in there but Lorimorning stayed over by the air intake for better air to breathe, while he made short forays over to clean and examine the structures better by the fire's light. He found a moving mechanism that probably could get removed, but then decided that there might be historical data that could be gathered here by scholars, so he left them as they were. There were plentiful containers, however, so he decided that many could be salvaged to be used for new purposes. He did keep one canister sealed with its hinge pin left in place, instead of cleaning out what surely was more long-decayed material inside. Scholars might find the mess useful, some day; he set it up by the access hole, to the side, however. It would be a long time before sufficiently wise scholars existed that could properly evaluate the contents of that canister, they speculated. There were many rows of canisters still on the racks, too.

They had found several connecting pins, fallen down inside the huge shell, under the meter diameter hole. It appeared that something on the inside had deliberately removed the cover from the inside, perhaps it had been the pilot of the vehicle. So they spent the rest of their allotted time here, digging debris that fell into the hole, carrying it out and dumping it outside, leaving only the steps and their fire hearth in place. They found what indeed must have been a seat for someone, perhaps a pilot, and it was close to where the vehicle was mangled by the impact. Any soft material that had been on the seat was long gone, but the framework of a seat was still clearly there. In front of it was a control panel; they rinsed the dirt off as much as possible, but there was not much to be identified. There were two grasping sticks with many parts, apparently the movement of each stick did something, and places for the thumb and four fingers each appeared to activate part of each grip. Each of them took turns sitting in the hard seat framework, grasped the two control sticks, tried to imagine what it was like to fly the vehicle. It seemed very advanced compared to the vehicles in town, yet it apparently was hundreds of years older. It probably had crashed even before any people lived on the planet, back when the planet was being first seeded with biological self-replicating seed-stock.

With some regret at having to leave this wondrous place, they packed up, he carrying two of the empty jars, she carrying the third one. They only had food enough for a snack on the hike back home; they had to leave now. They had not gathered the treasures that they had hoped they would find here; although the three lidded jars made of an amazing material, perhaps were a treasure in themselves. Remembering how long it took for Lorimorning to make the stone bowl that currently was their only means for heating a liquid, these three jars and their three lids would make six new containers for heating liquids. Or one container could keep its lid and be used for transporting water on a journey, perhaps. Treasures indeed.

It had gotten dark before they reached home, and Burtevertree had to use the hand crank flashlight to determine the pathway home the last part of the journey. He was glad that he had taken the time and effort to make a clear pathway through here. Finally they were back up into their cave home again, and soon with a cooking fire going in the hearth again, she prepared them a good meal, but still used just the stone bowl for cooking soup; she wanted to make sure the new jars were very clean before risking cooking or eating out of them.

After resting up a day, they made a trip over to their wooded homesite. The water had all drained from their lower room, but it was a mess. It all was still soggy, however, so they built over only half of the roof structure, by the time they headed back to the cave site. Back home in the cave, she declared that she did not want to make any more such trips, it was too tiring for her. So for the next several days, he went alone out to gather edibles and firewood, and cut an occasional special tree limb for building structures. And one day after he came back home with his gatherings, he found that the baby had been born; Lorimorning was nursing the child and asked him to use the stone bowl to heat water, then add some seeds and bits of dried meat into the water, let cook awhile then remove from the fire and when cool enough bring it over to her for her meal. When the stone bowl was emptied, he was told to do the same thing with water, seeds and bits of meat, and it was for his own meal. He said that was a lot of work just to eat something for a few minutes.

For the next couple of weeks he continued his scavenging for edibles and firewood and construction materials, working alone; while Lorimorning tended her newborn, and renewed her strength. She quickly recovered enough to resume cooking tasks, declaring that although Burtevertree could cook, she liked her own cooking better; he agreed, glad to be rid of the cooking job.

Deciding what would be the best uses for the three empty canisters they had brought back from the crashed seed ship, two of the lids were just too tempting for use as cooking and eating bowls, so that would require the two associated holding parts of the canisters, be open-topped. Still, they could hold water or seeds and nuts, as long as they were not moved a lot. The third canister was to be kept with its lid, thus could be used to carry edibles or drinking water on one's back while traversing the rough trails. These canisters were really welcome to them, additions to Lorimorning's carefully crafted baskets. That a canister could hold considerable drinking water for a long time, was especially welcome. After Lorimorning had heated them up very hot to clean them, Burtevertree took two of the canisters into the back cave and filled them with water from the cave's lake water, so they no longer would have to go there daily to drink and for cooking water in the stone bowl. With handy water at their cave home, he could then spend all day out scavenging for edibles and firewood, and occasionally also go work to restore the winter home.

A month after the baby was born, Lorimorning was getting urges to go do things again, so the three of them made a trip to the far end of the cave tunnel, to see what they could learn about their neighboring town's folks. Pulling away the brushwood from the opening of the cave, they were surprised to see several objects floating on the water, with people riding the floating objects, and pushing on the water using sticks. The two took turns peering out through the small opening, trading impressions with each other as to what was going on out there.

The floating objects the people were riding on, seemed to be carefully shaped wooden things, that had a pointed end that seemed to easily shove the water out of the way while the people used the sticks to propel around the lake. There appeared to be large floating objects and small ones; the small ones had smaller people on them, perhaps children. Sometimes one of the little people would leave a floating object, splash around in the water, then climb back into their floating object; why they did that was not obvious yet. Meanwhile the larger people stayed in their floating objects, and when they were not moving around, they seemed to wave a long thin pole around in the air, and sitting still for a long time afterwards. Occasionally one of them seemed to pull something out of the water and put it in the floating object.

Then Lorimorning declared that she had seen something move around in the water near them; it was long and dark yet shiny too as it moved; it never came up for air, either. Then it wiggled and the wiggling seemed to enable it to move away again, out of sight. Perhaps it was those things that the people in the floating objects were gathering from the water in the lake.

For the next couple of weeks, they made trips to the far end of the tunnel to watch what was going on, every couple of days. There were always some of the floating objects on the water and people in them. The children seemed to be able to splash around in the water and stay doing that for a long time, going far from their floating object sometimes.

Lorimorning was taking her turn at the peek hole when she suddenly exclaimed and jumped back. A child's face had appeared in the water right next to the opening. They could hear a child's voice saying "hello, hello." They had been discovered, apparently. There was no way to keep people of the lake from coming through this opening to wander the cave tunnel, and now that they had been discovered, by the child out there, what to do? Lorimorning made the decision and poked her head out the peek hole and said "hello" back, to the child, who was still doing a splashing and floating right in front of her. The child wanted to know who she was and why she was hiding in there. The children had been watching the peek hole for many days, seeing a face there at times, and were curious about what the game was.

17 MEETING THE LAKESIDE PEOPLE

Lorimorning said that they were from another town far away and were lost, and had made a home in the cave. That seemed to satisfy the child, who then swam over to one of the floating things, climbed on it, and used the stick to move away toward the others out in the lake.

Burtevertree wanted to know if they were dangerous or not; were they going to have to try to barricade the tunnel or even abandon their cave home to go live in their winter home quicker than had been planned. Lorimorning said the child did not look dangerous to her.

He took his turn looking out, and reported that several of the smaller floating objects with children on them, were now coming this direction, and one of the floating objects with an adult riding it, was also starting to move this way; but most of the people on the lake did not seem to change what they were doing. It did not look like a war party at this point. He backed out of the viewing hole, and Lorimorning wiggled in to look out again; there were three of the floating small objects in front of her, each with a child riding it, and a bit behind them was a larger floating object, with adults on it, a man and a woman. The children asked what game were they playing and how did they get in there, what was the place. The adults stared for awhile, then said that they did not recognize her. Also said that was a strange place for a person to be.

Lorimorning asked if the people were afraid of strangers, were they possibly dangerous. The man said they had not seen strangers before, but history told that there were other towns with people in them, far away. How did the strangers come so far and why did they do that? Lorimorning said that she and her husband had gotten lost long ago and had made a new home, and had found this tunnel that led to this place where they were watching what the people were doing out there in the water.

They all seemed friendly, but suddenly the children tore away the bushes from the cave opening, and eagerly were in the cave with Lorimorning, Burtevertree and the baby. The three children were eagerly exploring and chatting, one coming back and said it got too dark to see where the tunnel went.

The two adults asked if they too could come visit; Burtevertree agreed, so they too crawled in through the cave opening. The woman commented that there were no cooking or bedding items in here; yet it was dark further back in the cave. Lorimorning decided to take them all to their cave home; there was no other way to resolve this situation. Burtevertree cranked on the flashlight, lighting the way through the tunnel; they passed the area of collapsed access to the upper plateau, then on to the other cave entrance. Here the newcomers were very interested in how people could live this way. Apparently they had made everything here themselves.

Then they spotted the canisters. Inspecting them carefully, they asked what they were. Burtevertree said they had found them out in the forest area, and they were very helpful for storing things. Life here was primitive, and the canisters were a great help to them. The woman touched one of them, and then said she was a teacher, had studied the history, and said that the history was as handed down word of mouth until writing was created along with paper and ink. But what was written of history seemed to have many missing pieces. Could these canisters have anything to do with the Humming Wire? Burtevertree said he had never heard of a Humming Wire, and all the history where he was from, was just told verbally and taught by the town leaders, and no one was taught to write, although they could read a bit from the Tealers' old books. There never was any mention of a Humming Wire; but nothing of canisters either.

Lorimorning asked what was a Humming Wire, was it a musical instrument that people played? Could she see one? No, came the reply, the Humming Wire was a strange wire that was connected to a structure off in the distance, far from here; the Humming Wire was horizontal and seemed endless in both directions, and was along the same line as the sun circled the planet. The Humming Wire made a humming sound, was all that they could tell about it. History had guessed that it might be related to the creators that made all of this world.

The man was quite interested in the little external combustion engine, the generator and the lights. Burtevertree showed how it worked, by adding some water in the tank, then starting a fire under the tank, and soon the piston would be moving back and forth, cranking on the generator that made electricity that charged the battery and lit the lights in the cave. In the town, they too had electricity but it was generated by paddle-wheels in a waterfall. However, during parts of the year, there was not enough water in the waterfall to power all the generators, so only some uses of electricity were able to have power then. They had never seen an engine and that looked like something that could be made bigger, and could help add electrical power to their town in times of short waterfall energy.

The woman continued to be fascinated with the canisters, asking what they were used to hold. Water and food; could these not be also stored with ordinary containers made of metal or ceramics? If so, could they make a trade for one of the canisters?

Trading, they explained, was how all the couples in their town negotiated with the other couples. They traded goods and services. And now a trade was being offered, two ceramic containers, each able to hold as much water as one of these canisters, plus one metal barrel that would hold far more than a canister, plus two full sets of eating utensils, cups and plates, along with a cooking pot? Would that be a fair trade for the canister with a hinged lid?

Lorimorning quickly agreed to the trade; it sounded more than equal in value. It was explained that in town, the strange canister would be far more important as a historical item for their teaching museum, which was part of their schooling. There had never been anything like the canister before, and would bring much thought to the students. It was easily worth even more than the containers and utensils that had been offered. Now if they would be helped with the little light back to the lake entrance to the cave, then tomorrow they would again meet, and make an exchange for the complete canister.

On the way back to the lakeside cave opening, Burtevertree inquired about how people lived in the town on the other side of the lake. All the children were taught the same things; much of it was by observing and using the objects in the history museum, which also taught how paper was made, pen and ink, then the definitions of symbols for writing then reading what was written. As soon as the children began to become of schooling age, they were paired up as close friends, one boy with one girl, and they would associate for a month, then there would be a shift in who was with whom, so by the time years later when they passed the maturity ritual, they were quite familiar with how life was with many others of the opposite gender. They then paired up to fully live together, and would switch partners after several months. Two years later there would be a mass meeting and the young adults would choose among each other for a longer term relationship. this time for five years. However, there could be swaps between couples during that time, if people were finding that incompatibilities were surfacing. The marriages became declared more permanent as the years went by; but people changed their natural ways with time too, and so on rare situations, couples would swap partners for long term relationships. They were following the obvious principle that since about the same number of boys were born as were girls, that the creator clearly intended for them to pair up male plus female throughout life. But in practice they had found that compatibilities varied, thus the evaluations were going on in ever closer relationships between a man and a woman. Their prime way of being was that there would never be a time when a man and a woman were not together. Was that not the way in Burtevertree's town?

Lorimorning spoke up and diverted the trend of conversation a bit, saying that in the town where they had come from, life was very different. But they liked the ways of life in this new town by the lake, much better than the way of life where they had come from. She continued with saying that difficulties in the relationships of their former town, were what had caused their getting lost and the rugged life that they had lived since then. Was there opportunity for she and Burtevertree and the baby to live in the town across the lake?

There was silence to that for awhile, then the man carefully said that there had never been a stranger come to their town. Their society of paired individuals and their homes and resources, all tightly controlled by the trading protocols, had no place for anyone new that had not been of the town's children. Burtevertree suggested that the town's leaders might be able to arrange for new people, but the reply was that there were no town leaders; everybody led and followed equally, and the knowledge base was available to everybody equally, and so all people had an understanding of what needed to be done and simply stepped in to do what clearly was needed to be done in all ongoing situations.

No need for someone to tell them what to do; that kind of behavior was outlawed long ago, during a pivotal part of history when some men attempted to seize control of what other men did, and to take more than their share of the women. A conflict arose when two of the women had seen their husbands killed by the group of bosses, which explained the missing husbands of a couple of the other women in town. So all the women got together and demanded the group of bosses leave the town, and take no women with them.

There had been determined that the men who wanted to be bosses also sought to take a monopoly in breeding women, and worse, they did damage, and killed men who were not like them. The only way to obtain a peaceful cooperative constructive town was to eliminate those who had those destructive aggressive natures; the women refused to have any of those kind of children anymore. So they sent away the group of thirty men who had formed the boss group and had caused so much harm to others; there was something broken, wrong with that kind of man and too often they had passed those qualities on to their offspring.

It became part of the town's protocol set, that there be no bosses allowed, nor any taking of more than one mate at a time. Every adult always had a mate. In the situation where there were not enough to pair up with the opposite gender, some couples volunteered to take the extra in on their relationship sharing, so there were never any loners.

Lorimorning was thoughtful awhile, asked if that was correct, that there were thirty men of violent controlling nature who had been banished from their town - yes, there were thirty of them. And that had been two generations ago. Why did she ask? Lorimorning spoke slowly, still thinking of the implications. She replied that the town where she and Burtevertree came from, were ruled by a group of thirty men, and history said that the creator had sent thirty men to lead the town, and that was about two generations ago. Ever since then, it has been custom to have exactly thirty town leaders, all Tealer men, and who clearly were descendants of those original thirty men.

Lorimorning went on to say that in her town, whenever any man not of the town leaders, defied the decree that only the Tealer town leaders may mate with the women of the town, the town leaders would soon announce at the town meeting that that man had wanted women despite the creator's decree that only the town leaders may have intimacy with the women, so the man had left the town to go to a far town where there were plenty of women for them. Lorimorning had been getting to be good friends with Burtevertree, who was not a town leader, and then she was told that Burtevertree did not like her and he had left town to go to the far town where there were women for him.

So she felt sad and rejected, and then had accepted the town leaders as mates in the night. She had a lady-friend who suddenly said that she had been friends with a man and was her secret boyfriend, but she had just seen her boyfriend abducted by two of the town leaders, asking would Lorimorning go with her to find out what was happening. So the two women got in the back of the utility truck; they rode very uncomfortably in a pile of junk for many hours, then the truck stopped.

The women got out, sore and stiff, then saw the two Tealers taking her friend's boyfriend over to a cliff, his hands were tied and he was struggling a bit. The two women ran over to rescue the boyfriend, but in the struggle all five of them fell over the cliff.

She had awoken to see that it was a huge cliff that she was at the bottom of, and that she had a broken arm and leg, yet saved by being cushioned by the bodies of the others on top of which she had fallen onto at the bottom of the cliff. Her ladyfriend and her friend's boyfriend were killed by the huge fall, as were the two Tealer men.

Then she was rescued by Burtevertree, who had previously been thrown off the cliff by the same two town leader men, but his fall had been partially broken by a bush growing out of the cliff, and he had managed to heal and find ways to survive.

She realized that the town leaders had lied when saying that Burtevertree had chosen to leave town because he did not like Lorimorning; they had actually attempted to kill him. Worse, there were a great many human remains at the bottom of the cliff, some had been there for ages; so the abductions and disposal of men who did not choose to remain celibate had been going on for a very long time.

18 TRIP TO THE HUMMING WIRE

It appeared that the town leaders, the Tealers, were directly descended from the thirty men who had been banished from this very town by the lake. Indeed there was something broken about those thirty men, that drove them to prevent any other men besides their own kind from procreating, and they were actively harming others in the process. They also clearly were very deceptive, proclaiming to the town that they were declared supreme by the creator, and all the town must obey the town leaders.

And Lorimorning's child, a boy, was fathered by one of those town leaders, although she did not know which one, because several of them had visited her in the night over the months after Burtevertree had supposedly left town abandoning her.

Both Lorimorning and Burtevertree said that they liked the way of life in the town across the lake. And they understood how such a society needed to not be disturbed in the pairings and use of resources, no place for newcomers, especially tainted with the genetics of the men who were of violent polygamous conquering-urge nature. However, perhaps trading could happen more in the future. Lorimorning said that perhaps another of the canisters would be acceptable for further trade, and Burtevertree suggested that the technology for making the steam engine generator might be useful as a trade item. It was agreed that this new knowledge and opportunity could be spread among the townspeople, and some people would surely have comments about it all. It was agreed to meet again here at the lakeside cave entrance in a month, and decisions and perhaps trade offerings might be made then. As they were leaving, they handed Burtevertree a strange object, called a fish, and said it was good for food, please take it and enjoy as a gift.

Burtevertree could not carry all the new containers and utensils that had been traded with the people from the lakeside town, as they returned down the cave tunnel back home, so he carried the largest container, and in it he carried the strange thing called a fish, and also the two sets of dishes and eating utensils. It would be fine to have real plates and utensils again, but he hoped that Lorimorning would deal with the fish thing, which did not look edible to him.

Lorimorning had also bargained as part of the trade for the canister, for some of the things called paper, pen and ink. She had learned to read a little as taught by the town leaders, and she had seen books for teaching but none were given to anyone, nor were people taught to write. This new paper thing, and writing, was said to be a way to remember things, and to exchange information with others. She guessed that keeping such capabilities from the people of her town, enabled the town leaders to control the people better, since memories would fade and the town-leaders could then declare what had happened in the past. She shared some of the paper and writing instruments with Burtevertree, who had also been taught to read the town-leaders' books, but not taught to write; he learned to write a few words, then found it more interesting to sketch drawings on the paper.

He made a project to make a drawing of the cave tunnel system, counting the steps from one end to the other, and to its underground pond, and to the access hole to the top of the plateau. There were a couple of bends in the tunnel and he did his best to copy the angles in his drawing of the tunnel's location. As his skill progressed at this drawing, he estimated the distance in what might be a standard step-length, over to the seedship crash site, and also over to their underground home in the forest.

Another distance was added to the cliff-bottom where the remains of the truck was located along with the remains of a large number of people that the Tealers had thrown off the cliff, men who had been looking like they no longer would obey celibacy. Looked like hundreds of men had perished down there on the rocks. He and Lorimorning were fortunate to have survived; they found no indication that anybody else had done so, although some had apparently crawled off a few hundred meters then expired, too injured to go find food and water. It was a dismal place, and he made as few trips there to scavenge materials from the truck as possible.

His drawings of the distances and angles were a kind of map, drawn to satisfy some urge in himself. He added in the location of the cliff wall that surrounded the sunken valley, at least as much as he had traveled so far. His questions about the "humming wire" had pointed to a direction and distance from the lakeside entrance to the cave tunnel, were somewhat vaguely added to his increasingly complex map; and he had difficulty with some things seeming to cross over each other, his measurements were not accurate enough to prevent this. One of those apparent errors put the crash site of the ancient seed ship at the bottom of the cliff, while the location of the humming-wire apparently was about the same place, but was on a raised structure, the lake-city people said, near the edge of a canyon. Burtevertree was suspecting that the location of the humming-wire was at the top of the cliff below which was the seed ship. Both seemed to be artifacts of the creator's doings, that had placed life on this planet.

Meanwhile, Lorimorning's cooking expertise had proven that the fish was very tasty and nutritious. The three of them would occasionally go to the lakeside cave opening, and, using a "fishing pole" supplied by the lakeside town people, at times were able to bring back a fish, some for a couple meals and some was dried with other meat that Lorimorning was able to hunt with bow and arrow, up on top of the plateau.

On one of the hunting trips on top of the plateau, Burtevertree talked her into bringing along food and supplies for a three day stay up there, and he brought a tent he had made. He wanted to see if his estimate of where the humming-wire was, proved true. Besides, hunting the small animals could be done anywhere, and that path as good as any, he reasoned.

They encountered the humming-wire above them, long before reaching its anchoring point. First it was just heard, coming from above them, but nothing seen up there. as they got closer to the edge of the plateau, they could see a ribbon or wire stretching horizontally above them, with nothing holding it up, as far as they could see.

Another day's hiking and they came to the structure, looking much like how the lakeside town's people had described it; a stone-like tower broad at the base and narrower up higher, and through an aperture high in the tower, the humming wire was located. There was also a large kind of screen that stretched far across the land from the base of the tower; the screen was held up by many poles. Some of the trees had grown up through to be above the screen in places, but they seemed to have gotten scorched and did not grow much higher. They grew well where they were under the screen, however, as did the underbrush.

Burtevertree cautiously peered over the edge of the cliff, down into the canyon, trying to see if indeed the crashed seedship was down there. But it was a hugely deep canyon wall, and objects far down there were not clear to see; it was just forest. He had brought along a brightly colored cloth, and dangled it a bit over the side of the canyon, and fastened down its tether rope. He could attempt to see the object from below, next trip to the seed ship. The humming-wire extended out over the canyon, seemed to go in a straight line horizontally as far as it could be seen; it was a very strange thing.

He added in all this onto his maps; this was satisfying for him to achieve. Observing the humming-wire on one side of the opening in the tower, it seemed that the humming-wire vibrated a bit more than it did on the other side of the tower, He also reasoned that the humming-wire was stretched very tight and it was moving through the air at a high rate of speed. If so, that meant that the humming-wire extended a long distance from here, in both directions.

Meanwhile, Lorimorning was practicing writing, copying words out of the one book she had gotten from the lakeside town's people. And increasingly what she wrote was a story of where they went and what they did. It was a rough description, since her vocabulary was little, but at times it did help her remember things better.

The drinking water that they carried was getting low, so they packed up and headed back the way they came; by nightfall they had found the hole down into their cave tunnel, and by the light of the hand-crank flashlight, they traveled the tunnel, first filling their water jug at the underground pond. It was nice to rest at home, bright light in the cave home from the battery, and Lorimorning cooked them a good meal, and she prepared some of the animal meat to dry for later meals.

After resting up a couple of days, they again went to the lake end of the cave tunnel to fish and see if some of their new friends would come over to visit with them. Soon two couples came over in the floating things they called boats.

Lorimorning wanted more writing supplies. What did they have to trade, it was asked. By this time all three of their seed canisters had been traded to the lakeside town's people. Finally Burtevertree asked if they would consider new knowledge worth trading for. The answer was that usually knowledge was traded in kind, knowledge for knowledge. But there was little new knowledge not known by the townspeople anymore, and their education system taught everybody all the knowledge that had been accumulated in their writings.

Burtevertree than tested his skill at the trading game. He declared that he owned the remains of a crashed ancient seed ship, and he would trade, for a substantial amount of writing supplies, giving an adventure to the two couples, taking them over to see and go inside the crashed strange vehicle. A deal was struck; the two couples would return over at the cave opening in two days, bringing half of the agreed-upon writing supplies, plus their own hiking supplies for the journey.

19 CRASHED SEEDSHIP INDEED

Meeting at the cave's lakeside entrance two days later, the two boats were tied to brush near the cave entrance; and the seven of them traveled to the cave home at the other end of the tunnel, where they rested and ate. Then they all followed Burtevertree and Lorimorning with their infant along the primitive path he had built between the cave and the seed ship site.

As they got closer to the seed ship site, Burtevertree would occasionally pause and look up toward the top of the cliff wall towering high above them. Finally he saw it, the brightly colored cloth he had dangled over the side of the canyon, next to where the humming-wire's tower was located. He pointed the bright object out to the newcomers, and told what the bright object was, and that it was located close to where the humming-wire's tower was located.

By the time they got to the hole in the ground next to the base of the cliff, it was clear that it was directly below where the bright cloth was located, and thus was right below the humming-wire's tower location far above on top of the cliff.

Then lighting a torch, he took the newcomers down inside the strange structure, pointing out the odd material of its outside shell. He showed them the seat and what apparently was the control panel, which he and Lorimorning had carefully rinsed off and cleaned; but other than odd shapes and surfaces, nothing could be determined as to function. But it was clear that it had been some kind of machine, probably a vehicle; but how it got here or why, was not apparent. There was an unopened canister sitting up there, which Burtevertree had brought up and placed there; he pointed it out to the newcomers, and suggested that the town's scholars might be interested in its contents, as well as having another of the ancient canisters; what would they trade for it?

They agreed that all knowledge about the contents of the canister would be shared as part of the trade, and the contents plus the canister would be kept as future payment of trade, until its value was paid up. Meanwhile, one of the newcomers drew sketches of the vehicle, particularly of the seat and control panel; Burtevertree was fascinated by the skill that was displayed in the artistry that made a picture almost as if the objects themselves were seen. Could Burtevertree be taught the skill of making such a visual representation? Maybe, they could try, but it was a skill normally taught when children were very young and thus more easily learned new skills. But they would teach him as much as he could learn, anyway.

The newcomers thought that the crash that had made the hole through which they had entered, must have broken off pieces of the shell of the seed ship, and that they would very much like to take back one of those pieces of this strange material. Burtevertree said he thought it was foamed nickel-iron steel and ceramic, but how that was made was unknown. All attempts to lighten nickel-iron steel by having it cool while containing bubbles, had failed. Gravity seemed to prevent such a material to be made; but here it was, and nicely made, too. If they could find enough pieces of the material, a small piece could be heated to the melting point of meteor nickel-iron, and most likely it would just melt into a thin puddle, losing all the bubbles inside. All of them except Lorimorning took turns using the shovel that Burtevertree had made and had left here. They dug carefully in the volume of debris just under the hole in the vehicle, sending the diggings up to others outside where it could be examined carefully, and carefully placed aside in an identifiable area for later further analysis. If this indeed was one of the fabled seedships from before humans had been brought here to set up the towns, it was ancient indeed. It held knowledge that people had only guessed at, or was carried by word of mouth until writing on paper had been invented. Each shovel-full was carried up to the surface as if it were a treasure. But up there it just looked like ordinary forest floor debris, along with some stone shards from the cliff face.

There was a lot of debris to be dug out, and they needed to leave soon to get back before dark. They decided to dig right next to the inside shell surface for the last few shovelfuls, seemed more likely to find bits of the broken vehicle there. And with the last shovel-full they dared permit themselves for today, they found an object, crusted in mud, probably not a piece of the vehicle's exterior, but clearly not a natural object. Burtevertree and Lorimorning claimed this whole seed ship as belonging to them, and if the newcomer lakeside town folk were willing, they would be willing to trade the object for comparable value items. They already had established that the lakeside town's folks were very honest and fair in their trading arranging arrangements. It was agreed, a trade made, and value to be determined later by the lakeside town's folk; part of it would be to share knowledge that was gained, with Burtevertree and Lorimorning.

They hastily broke camp and headed back along the trail, led by Burtevertree since he had made the trail, although he claimed that Lorimorning's hunter abilities might be better at finding their way home if it got dark before they got back to the cave entrance. They had to make a small torch from forest deadwood, lit by the fire-start that Burtevertree carried on his belt, to find the way the last hour of the hike back. Finally they were back in the cave home, lit with the electric lights. All rested there awhile, eating food they had brought along, to conserve the food stored in the cave. Then they all walked the cave path, lit by the hand-crank flashlight. Finally they got to the lakeside opening of the tunnel, but realized they had no way to find their way across the lake in the dark, on their boats.

Breaking off some nearby deadwood from the brush at the cave entrance, Burtevertree made a small torch, lit again from the glowing fire-start he carried. He made two more small bundles of brush twigs, including some bigger pieces, as large as he could break off. He suggested that one of the couples start paddling toward the star pattern which they knew was in the direction where their town was, referenced to the cave opening. The other couple would follow right behind, watching the glow of the torch in the lead boat. When the torch was nearing its end, they would light the second bundle, new torch. And later the third bundle if needed. If all the torches had burned out before getting to the far shore, then they would independently paddle in the direction of the star pattern in the night.

They all agreed to meet at the cave entrance in three days from now; and the two boats went off into the night. Burtevertree, Lorimorning and the baby watched until they could no longer see the glow of the torch; then they headed back down the long tunnel, taking turns cranking on the flashlight.

They chatted as they went along. Lorimorning liked to talk about her toddler; he already was showing the distinctive physical characteristics of the Tealer town leaders, in color of hair and facial features. She was sure he was big for his age, like the town leaders were. She was carefully breaking Burtevertree into the situation of raising a member of the Tealer kind, and finding ways to integrate the bossy arrogant and uncannily aware personality that the child would most likely become. Lorimorning also broke the news that she was expecting again, this time would be Burtevertree's offspring, just as she had promised. No doubt this new child would be quite different from the infant. Yet they needed many kinds of qualities and characteristics, to set up a viable community that would outlive them. Maybe the lakeside town's folks would eventually accept them, but at this point, it did not look likely to happen.

Lorimorning explained that among the womenfolk of her town, there was still history that was handed down word of mouth, that was in addition to the history as taught by the town-leaders. This additional knowledge enabled much to be comprehensible. For example, the town only had the four truck vehicles. One had been lost through Burtevertree's efforts. The other trucks might be considered too valuable to send looking for the other truck and the two missing town leaders that had driven it to dispose of another non-celibate male.

It was easily clear to the town's womenfolk. Although the new town's leaders, who had come from supposedly the creator to populate the town, were uncanny in detecting when each woman was fertile, and would hound her until after her fertile time, spending nights with her, some of the women still managed to procreate with the remaining men of the original town's composition. It was about 9 children by the Tealer town-leaders to 1 child by the original male lineage of the town. Each generation had seen fewer of the original male lineage. Burtevertree was clearly of the original lineage, and was probably why he was selected to be thrown off the cliff; the town-leaders wanted to eliminate all genes of the original males of the town. Why they wanted to do that was a mystery to the women of the town; it was part of what was broken yet powerful in the town leader males.

One of the effects was that the skills and aptitudes were lost that were needed to build and maintain the trucks, was part of the original males of the town; the town-leaders seemed to have no ability to do the metallurgy, engineering and craftsmanship needed to build or maintain the trucks. The males of the town-leader genetics were incredibly skilled at getting other people to obey them. But as for building things, they were incompetent. And they had about eliminated the builder-genes of the town, by eliminating the genes of the original males of the town. The male genes of the town-leaders built males who were larger and more physically powerful in combat, and seemed to have no restraints as to the damage or hurt they did to others, in their efforts to force others to do what was directed by the town-leaders.

The womenfolk of the town realized that the near total loss of the original male genes in the town, was also eliminating the town's ability to build and maintain what was needed for survival. But the town-leader males were ever watching and controlling the women and the males not of their elite group, and they were uncanny in the observational skill as well as utterly brutal in their responses if they found any who were not obeying. Those qualities were probably how the lakeside town folk identified them and then banished them from town.

Unfortunately, instead of vanishing with no way to procreate, the gang of powerful brutal and uncannily observant males had found Lorimorning's and Burtevertree's ancestral town, and ever since was using it to make more copies of the elite Tealer town-leaders. That urge apparently was part of their genes, and enabled them to reproduce despite being unable to help in the survival of the people. They were a kind of parasite on humanity.

She and Burtevertree now had a chance to procreate often and bring back the ancestral genes of their town of origin, able to build trucks again, she hoped. But they also had her firstborn, clearly one of the Tealer genetics. She hoped that they could somehow get him to blend in and be helpful. But the experience of the lakeside town's people had suggested that was not possible. But now the two of them needed to try anyway. She considered the male toddler a beloved, whatever.

Burtevertree had been silent along the long tunnel, listening to her chatter. When she was silent a long time, he commented that nothing about this existence in this valley had been easy, and what she had intimated as what would be a difficulty, seemed to him just another factor to be in the picture.

Lorimorning was both relieved at that comment, and yet disturbed too. She replied that was a welcome attitude. Yet, he needed to remember, it was that attitude also of the original males of their ancestral town, and had ignored the impulses of the invading town-leader type that had almost killed off all the males of the town. It might be a bit harder problem than he realized. Yet she was glad he was taking on the task.

James E. D. Cline

20 ARCHAEOLOGICAL DIG

Several days later, as agreed with the lakeside town's pair of couples, they got together in the lake cave entrance at dawn, in time to relax a bit, have a snack and to do a little fishing. But as soon as it got light enough to swing out the fishing poles, suddenly there were a lot of boats converging on their location. Two of them had bright lights suspended high in the air, helping guide the others. The first couples to arrive assured that this was not an invasion; the genes of that kind had been cast out when they banished the Tealer bunch that had unfortunately taken over Burtevertree's town long ago. What these people wanted to do was to share in the adventure of exploring one of the fabled seed-ships of the creators. They had brought along lights that were powered by small batteries that were recharged by occasional hand-cranking; these would enable easier traversing of the cave tunnel, across the path through the forest to the site of the seed ship's remains, and to explore the seed ship more thoroughly, day or night, inside or out. They also brought digging and sifting tools, along with people to write and draw all that was happening for the history. This was a great time. Would it be permitted for them to accompany Burtevertree and Lorimorning and the toddler, on this time of great discovery that they could help do?

It was an offer that could not be refused. No fishing to be done today; they all began the long journey down the tunnel, this time lit by the helpers with their brighter lights. Lorimorning suggested that they would like to trade for one of the battery powered hand crank lights, an improvement over their one hand-crank light. With the steady light from the two new lights, despite the large number of people, they got to the cave entrance faster than usual. This time there was neither room for all the people, nor any interest by the new crowd, to stop for refreshments; they wanted to push on to the crash site right away.

Lorimorning quickly prepared some food and water for the three of them, while Burtevertree gathered a small portable shelter and his best digging tools. And then they led the group down the path, which was getting fairly well marked now by all the trampling along it.

When they got to the seed ship's crash site, it appeared that the organization of the pairs of people from the lakeside town, was quite efficient and had apparently been coordinated by plans before they got there. After getting permission from Burtevertree, the group began an archaeological dig protocol, carefully identifying original locations on a 3-D drawing, then each shovelful was lifted up out of the opening to the folks stationed above, who carefully sifted through the debris, writing down all that was observed, and separating out the components of the shovelful, whether dirt, twigs, or possible particles from the seed ship. Quite a well organized and coordinated process going on, yet without any apparent manager or overall management person giving orders. Burtevertree was very impressed, having only known the organization of efforts by the Tealer Town Leaders managing everything that was done by people. Including managing reproduction - the town-leaders were the only men allowed to reproduce - but here, all were already paired up, each man with a woman, and they worked in harmony both together and also as a paired team with the overall group. Nicely done, he thought. Yet he wondered, how did they do it. He only knew of the orders from the Town Leaders; although, he and Lorimorning had figured out very workable ways for them to work together as a team with no outside management.

With so many people efficiently working on the project together, progress was rapid. They had removed perhaps half of the debris from the control area of the seed ship by nightfall; they all took a dinner break from the supplies they had brought along; then they worked several hours more, helped by the light of one battery powered light inside, and the other light for the above-ground sifting and documenting group.

Finally all the lakeside town folks went aboveground, set up their portable hovels, and retired to dinner and sleep, leaving Lorimorning and Burtevertree to fend for themselves; clearly, all couples provided for their own needs, in the way of the lakeside folks. Although Burtevertree had brought along a tent for them to sleep in, it seemed easier to simply set up home inside the seedship. They first had a meal by light of a torch, then set up a sleeping area by light of their hand-crank light. Wearily, the three of them slept; it was fairly comfortable in their bedding brought along, using the tent as a bottom layer.

They were awakened by a light brought down by the new folks; they said it would be light outside in half an hour, and would they please accept food and drink as provided by the townsfolk, as breakfast to prepare for a busy day. Lorimorning was quite willing to have food from someone else already prepared for breakfast; but when she found out that it was raw fish she still had to cook, well, she dealt with it. And they agreed that the fish, with spices from the town, was a very fine breakfast, unusual for them or not.

As predicted by the townsfolk, light was coming in through the hole in the top of the crashed vehicle by the time they had finished the unusual but tasty meal. Then the lakeside town folk pairs began their routine same as yesterday, at first working in light assisted by the hand-crank-recharged batteries, until the sunshine was enough to work above ground well enough.

By midday they had cleaned out the entire control area of the vehicle and were rinsing off all the internal surfaces. They said they were also making progress unearthing the exterior of the vehicle at the same time. The artists were busy making drawings of the internal surfaces, although only the exterior of the control surfaces was visible; whatever had enlivened the instrument panel, was not doing so at this time.

Regretting that he would have to reveal the huge supply of canisters when allowing the newcomers to continue their clearing out of the vehicle, Burtevertree led some of the newcomers down into the lower areas, showed them the opening porthole in the side of the vehicle, and suggested bailing out the water, which had somewhat refilled by then.

The newcomers brought down a couple of metal cooking containers from their dishes, and began bailing water out, pouring the water out the porthole. In an hour they had again exposed rows of canisters that had been underwater; Burtevertree then explained that this was where they had gotten the first of the canisters, which they had now traded to the lakeside town's folks. If the lakeside townsfolk wanted to take more of the canisters from here, they would need to trade for them; and part of the trade would be knowledge and usefulness of whatever was discovered by the contents of the canisters. The first three canister's contents he had originally discarded onto the forest floor, was perhaps regrettable but did provide impetus for what was transpiring now.

The analysis of the first unopened canister's contents by the experts historians and scientists of the lakeside town-folks, had found that the contents had decomposed to a stable population of microbiota; nothing had survived of the seeds genetics. But it was yet to be determined if that was generally true of all these seed canisters from so long ago. The historians of the town would like to trade for many of the sealed canisters, for future research, and some to be kept sealed for use by possible future more competent science facilities. But they would like to leave most of the canisters right where they are now; this was a historical site of great significance, even if they did not now understand it all.

The bailing out of the water continued with many laborers, but at some point, seepage from somewhere was filing the volume as fast as water could be removed. So at that point, both lights were brought down, people scrubbed off the scum from the surfaces, and the artists made quick sketches of what was observed. The mechanisms for bringing the canisters around along the racks was easy to see, but where they were dumped had yet to be seen. Perhaps that opening was where the water was coming in, from the forest springtime melt, still subsiding.

That there had been only one human-seating framework in the whole vehicle, at least the part they had cleared at this point, was of interest. No human remains had been found in the debris inside the vehicle, so it was agreed that the pilot had probably left the vehicle through the porthole. And if this was at the time before vegetation had established itself on the planet, the pilot would either need to be rescued by someone, or had perished quickly, no nourishment nor companionship yet existing here. They briefly fantasized the fate of the pilot, and felt sorrow; yet, it had enabled the lives of all who had gathered here for this discovery from the past. The effort had not been wasted. Perhaps the skeleton of the pilot was out there, somewhere now overgrown by the abundant forest foliage. If so, it was surely quite hidden from them; perhaps some future generation of scientists would find the remains.

21 NEW SEEDS AND MAPS

So, what had happened to cause the crash, and what was the progression of destruction? What were the losses to the planet regarding the lack of what this seedship had carried? And could they use the decomposed remains of some of the canisters, to re-create the missing flora. With this summary, the archaeological group packed up, headed back down the forest trail, bringing several canisters, as well as many bags of siftings. They had found many fragments of the outer shell of the seedship, and would be analyzed and provide new museum artifacts for all to admire.

Once again the crowd just walked right through the cave entrance home, and continued down the long upward tunnel, to exit at the lakeside cave opening. As they left, the lakeside town's couples said that they would provide a summary of trade value, after evaluating what they brought back home from this research journey. All results would be shared with Burtevertree and Lorimorning. They would return in three days, meet here; that would give them time to rest up, make some initial evaluations of the new findings.

Lorimorning ruefully declared that this cave entrance home was becoming a thoroughfare for the lakeside town's people. Nice people that they were, there was no room for a comfortable home here at the same time as being a big pathway for others whenever they chose.

Burtevertree thought about it and then agreed. More thought, and he suggested they could build an extension to the cave entrance, out from it, built using tree branches. Maybe be able to use some shards of the cliff face as part of it. Perhaps could become a year-around residence for them, and enable connection with their new trade folk who seemed benign, and had connection to their own heritage town.

However, there seemed to be no clear answer to their problem. Maybe they could endure the invasions for awhile then declare the crash site off limits for access by the lakeside people, once they had finished their main field research tasks there. Otherwise the seedship's remains might become a part of the town's "museum" of education.

Lorimorning decided that they ought to put all their effort into building their winter home, this time including a raised section that would not flood in springtime, where they could live year around. She also wanted to clear a space near there, in which to plant a garden, to concentrate edibles.

They made a trip by themselves over to the seed ship site, bringing back two of the canisters from inside it. There appeared to be hundreds of them in there, and some still submerged below the water level inside the wreck. They took these two canisters directly to their planned year-around homesite, as the canisters would be welcome water storage containers; and they planned to utilize the contents of the canisters in a side area of their planned garden. The canisters had a decayed mess inside, but which might still have some beneficial soil biosystem bacteria that had not been seeded yet and might help grow food.

They decided on a garden area, clearing all vegetation from it, saving all the tree and brush material to the side for their upcoming construction. They opened up the first canister, spread its contents along one edge of the garden, turning some under the soil surface. Then they opened the second canister and were surprised that it was not a mess inside, but was clearly a single type of seed; it apparently either did not need some accompanying bacteria, or else was not vulnerable in storage to decay, so it had apparently been carefully prepared. They poured out a handful of the seeds, then re-sealed the canister; the seeds might be important in the future ecosystem. It might be an already common plant that had missed being seeded on some far place on the planet, but they did not recognize the seed from the plants they had seen before. They thoughtfully planted several of the new seeds on the edge of their new garden site.

They took the emptied canister over to the nearest spring, rinsed it well and filled it with water. Back to their construction site, poured a little water on their new plantings, then they began the construction of the raised platform, which was to be built into the tree under which the survival site had originally been built. The tree provided solid mounting in some areas, and would provide some concealment, perhaps. What the future held was uncertain.

A few days later, they returned to the seed ship site, and brought back two more of the sealed canisters; there were plenty of them, and they thought two more sealed drinking water carriers would be needed, although up until now, there had been springs in the area to get drinking water. But what if they got sick awhile and could not forage? Stored supplies seemed an important part of their rebuilt and expanded home out here in the forest.

An agreement was made with the lakeside townspeople, that they would have status as ever invited guests, able to utilize the long cave tunnel to access the seedship crash site as part of their research and museum-education system. In return, some tools would be provided by the lakeside folks, things like metal shovels and saws, hammers and nails, more food storage and cooking utensils, that would be occasionally brought and left at the cave entrance.

Months went by in which the raised section of their forest home became quite livable and now had the steam engine, generator and lighting system moved into it. All their cave entrance home's main living stuff was moved to the raised platform part of their forest home, except a token amount of items for some storage and food preparation was left on the side of the cave, more to remind folks that it was still a potential living space for the newcomers in the valley down here.

Lorimorning's toddler became skilled and obedient, and when Lorimorning gave birth to her first child by Burtevertree, the first little boy was quite active, helpful at times, but clearly with a somewhat different kind of personality than was characteristic of Lorimorning, Burtevertree or even of any of the lakeside folks. The little boy looked a bit different and hair color same as that of the former Tealer town leaders, yet also he seemed to require an assigned social status place, a chain of command where he knew where he fit. He also seemed to have an uncanny sense about some things, which puzzled Lorimorning yet slowly saw similarities to the Town Leader men who had educated her and had later visited her in the nights. They all seemed to not only be bigger and ready to physically assault, they also had an uncanny sense of what others were going to do, as well as where to find things that were out of sight; they also seemed to always have a pre-planned coordinated system of events by which they lived and ruled the town. Maybe those were genetic things instead of learned ways of being, she wondered, discussing it with Burtevertree.

But unknown to them, the former home's Town Leaders were also concerned. They were sure that they were born to rule the world, and it was not just their superior strength and willingness to harm other people, and their teamwork, but their ability to be aware of things at a distance, that would enable their rule of everything. They could send a part of their etheric self to go see beyond where their physical body's senses were located, for one thing; they could send this etheric self to merge with another person and experience what that person was experiencing to some extent. This enabled much of their ability to rule, because it enabled them to become aware what any potential rivals were doing to compete with the Town Leaders. It also enabled them to identify which males that had been born that were not of Tealer genetics, who did not want to remain celibate; clearly some of that was going on as the women still occasionally had one of those original type male babies, like Burtevertree had been. And right now, the town Leaders were aware of a new boy born of their kind, but which was located far away, living with Lorimorning and Burtevertree. They would need to somehow get the boy back to be amongst the Town Leaders, since he clearly had well-developed etheric body awareness abilities, and would be fitting to be among the thirty Town Leadership some day.

The Tealer Town Leaders had male genetics that were very different from most humans. They knew from birth they were born to rule everything. As they grew up, they constantly interacted with other people, their own kind especially, ever testing to see where they were on the distribution of how fast they could run, how high could jump, how violently to hit, how trickily to deceive, and how well to use their etheric body self to go peer at what an opponent was up to and to also influence the opponent to do something at a specific time, and thus be easily defeated. Their world was made up of their own male kind and the swirl of their constant interactions, and being obedient to their location in the complex status arrangement of who was boss of whom among themselves. When they had to encounter a person who was not as skilled at their unique rulership ways, they easily tricked, internally sabotaged or physically knocked down any who did not obey them. Simple as that.

But they had the problem, that in using the women of this town to breed more of their own kind of male, the original kind of male was becoming extinct; and those were the kind who were able to build things like the trucks in which the Town Leaders depended on for many of their activities. They were frustrated that men who only had half of the Town Leader qualities still could not comprehend how to build things and keep them working. The town's resources were therefore slowly wearing out; some of the women could do some of the constructive tasks, but not with the keen expertise exhibited by the former men of their kind.

But when it came to conquering a whole town, sometimes it was not so easy, as they had found when the lakeside townsfolk would not tolerate the badgering by the born-ruler type aggressive snoopy men, and had cast them out of their town. By the time the Tealers had located and entered this town, they had decided to try a more deceptive technique, and it was working quite well; most of the males out in the community were now at least partially of the born-ruler genetics, Only the purest of the born-ruler genetics were accepted into the thirty Town Leader group; all other males of the town were taught that celibacy was the only way to be acceptable in the town. Women who wanted progeny thus needed to be receiving the Town Leader men as mates; thus more likely to produce the genetics sought by the Tealer Town Leaders. They needed more men, however, because to get the broader functions provided by a town, such as building things, they were going to have to go back to the lakeside town and overwhelm it by force in a surprise attack.

Losing Lorimorning and her girlfriend was a loss in reproductive capability, yet the hidden trick of using their etheric body to go see and manipulate beyond their physical body, they knew Lorimorning had born that child fathered by the Town Leaders before she had escaped. The boy was a needed resource of the Town Leaders, but they did not know how to retrieve him.

At the same time as they lost the two women, they had also lost two of their own, along with a truck. The same two of the Town Leaders who had been disposing of the non-celibate men of the larger town for decades, and who were the only ones who knew exactly how that disposal was done or where it was done. They chose the best two genetically superior men from town, accepting them into the Town Leaders to restore their number to thirty, but it would take time to indoctrinate them into full consensus with the more experienced members. So they sent out two men in one of the remaining trucks, with instructions to explore the paths of the nearby roads; they would drive for only half an hour, then return, to make sure they did not get lost.

However, the consensus was that the abduction and disposal trip made by the now-missing members, had always taken over four hours to do. The events were always timed to snatch the target man when no people would observe it happening, and then the victim would be taken directly to be disposed of, then the two would return in the truck, and this process had always taken four or more hours, so it seemed likely that where they had gone was a lot farther than was being explored now. Still, the half hour distance drives were gathering experience in driving the rough roads, seeing what was out there, being able to get back home.

They made maps using the paper in the back of the books that they had taken from these townsfolk when they first took over the town a couple generations ago; using drawing pens was still something the Town leaders were able to do, even though they forbade the larger community of people of the town, including the students, from drawing or writing. Each drive in the truck yielded a new map, and the first few weeks of trips were to do the exact same trip; eventually all the resulting paper maps were combined to make a final map. There were three roads connecting to the town, and they had explored all three out to the half-hour-drive distance for this map. So from there, they picked one road, and traveled it out an additional half hour; repeating that trip yielded an extension of the final map.

It took them a couple years to reach the point of a map that had gone three hours on each of the roads. This ought to have gone farther than the missing tuck had gone in two hours, yet the truck was never seen.

22   OF TRACKS AND TEACHING

The lakeside town folk worriedly advised Burtevertree that their vibration sensors had detected the rumble of trucks along the road again, and for awhile it seemed fairly regular, one a week for several months.

So he took one of the couples to the place in the cave tunnel where it opened to the top of the plateau, and from there over to the road. Yes, the road was being pounded down again by truck tires. He suspected that the missing truck was the target of the trips; fortunately the truck was no longer up here. But the poorly hidden pile of things they had removed from their victims before tossing the people over the cliff, was still in the brush near the edge of the cliff. If the stuff was discovered, then they would look over the cliff and find the remains of the truck below, and thus know where to hunt for he and Lorimorning.

They were attempting to conceal their own tracks, but did not have ways to do that well; the Town Leader men were uncanny in their perceptions too. Crossing the road's many tire tracks on the way to toss the stuff over the cliff, would leave a trace of having been here; and what if the truck happened to be out this way while they were up here doing that.

So Burtevertree decided that they ought to just leave the stuff over there for now, backtrack to the hole in the ground leading to the cave tunnel, using a branch of a bush to sweep their trail a bit in hopes of erasing remains of their presence. It seemed that they all needed to prepare for conflict with the born-ruler men and a army of half-breeds fighting with them.

The lakeside folks assigned four couples to come to visit Burtevertree and Lorimorning every other day, to gather knowledge about the ways of the town that had been taken over by the cast-out Tealer born-leaders. What would be the resources available to the Town Leaders in setting up an invasion, and what would they be seeking at first.

Burtevertree suggested maybe setting up a trade system would provide a way to prevent extreme conflict, but the lakeside townsfolk sadly told of the apparently inborn qualities of the born-ruler men's kind, that they incorrigibly craved to rule other people, even more than to have resources.

The lakeside town's people also advised Lorimorning that, since the more similar something is to another thing and the more complex they similarly are, the more they are connected despite spatial separation. This seemed especially strong in the type of person that had to be ousted from the lakeside town, since that genetics both craved to force other people to do as was demanded, but also all those genetic folks were very strongly linked as similar and seemed to be able to communicate with each other at some level all the time. They proclaimed it was their male ancestral genes that enabled them to have such an uncanny way of observing beyond their physical senses, but also to be able to influence things beyond themselves.

All people had some of this capacity, but normally had less similar male genetics, being more diverse; and normally did not have the urge to violently coerce other people. The effect was part of what was taught in the lakeside town's museum education system, along with other ways to observe and measure and manipulate things on a more physical level in the sciences.

The caution was that Lorimorning's first son, fathered by one of the Tealer Town Leader type of male before she came to be with Burtevertree, was almost certainly connected with the Town Leaders on the level of similarities, and would be aware of each other to some extent, more-so the older he got. It was possible that he would be used to find Lorimorning so as to abduct her and take her back to breed more of the Town Leader coercive men, while also taking her son to be brought up as a Town Leader candidate. They would not likely leave Burtevertree alive, either.

The lakeside town folks did not think they would be more of a danger to themselves, since surely the Town Leader men already knew how to get back to the lakeside town from where their ancestors were banished many decades in the past. The lakeside town's folks were aware of the danger, however, thanks to the presence of Lorimorning and Burtevertree, having told them of the fate of their town having been taken over by the group of ousted Town Leaders, who have been eradicating the original male genes from the town, through their demands that all men except themselves be celibate. And the Town Leaders had the mysterious way of somehow observing any man or woman disobeying; the Town Leaders taught that it was a great invisible power that ruled above all, and helped the Town Leaders rule, and had also demanded that males without a strong dose of the Town Leader genetics, be celibate. That the Town Leaders inborn craving to rule all other people and thus own all there was, were breeding an army for conquering, was evident. The lakeside town's folk apologized for setting them loose on the world, ousting them as a group, thinking they would perish without women with which to breed; but the reverse had happened.

The lakeside town's folk have the fine system of always pairing up male and female as the primary unit amongst themselves; it made for a fine development of their educational system and their growing industrial and agricultural capacity. But it did not enable them to be very good at being warriors. They now knew they had to develop some capacity for defending themselves, both from an assault by an army of Town Leader type men, or else by having the outskirts of their agricultural area being at risk of having couples snatched by lurking Town Leader men, killing the men and taking the women for breeding. They similarly had no resources for defending the valley here where Lorimorning and Burtevertree lived and were creating a family.

Burtevertree grumped that life here was already a struggle for survival; and to also have to worry about invasion by the men who had already tried to kill him, seemed almost overwhelming. It seemed wise to somehow conceal and seal the opening that led to the top of the plateau, and do that as soon as possible. It would be a loss that Lorimorning could no longer use that route to hunt for the small animals up there for part of their food; but they now were raising two kinds of the animals in pens down here in the valley, so that would help assure a future source of that food. They also had set loose a few of the animals of one kind, to live elsewhere in the valley range.

The lakeside town's folks pitched in to help brush away traces of the access paths to the cave opening, backtracking to the opening down into the cave tunnel. Then they built a stone arch out of rock shards from the base of the cliffs in the valley, through which they would still be able to go through the cave tunnel; then on top of this stone archway they moved the fallen dirt in the tunnel, onto the top of the archway, filling up to the opening on the plateau's surface. Transplanting a couple of brush plants onto the top of the filled-in hole, they plugged the last of the dirt from below, best they could do. The remaining indentation would hopefully be concealed by the growing brush. If it were a few years before the area was being looked over by the Town Leader people, the weather ought to finish erasing traces of the access hole that had led down to the cave tunnel's access of the valley floor and thus to Burtevertree and Lorimorning's cave entrance homesite.

But Lorimorning's first son would surely be something of a beacon to their location, and both she and Burtevertree were very protective of the boy, and would not consider releasing him to the wild on top of the plateau for the Town Leaders to find and take away. The boy was part of their family, and would remain so. The lakeside town's folks were invited to help with the boy's education and to study him at the same time, but they were not allowed to teach him of the risks of his special urges that would surely develop as he matured, same as did the males of that type among the lakeside town's folks before their ousting decades ago.

However, both Lorimorning and Burtevertree declared that, now knowing the nature of the problem, that they would strive to teach the boy better ways to use those aggressive urges to uncannily stalk and assault other men. Burtevertree remembered that while all boys were growing up together, being taught by the Town Leaders, that those boys with those Town Leader qualities, were also, as boys, ever busily playing all kinds of team games with each other; they easily beat any of the boys that were not of their kind, when any wanted to join in on the fun of the games.

So Burtevertree sought to play games with the boy, games Burtevertree made up; and these games always involved contests of building things and taking them apart carefully to build something new with the pieces. The boy seemed interested in participating in these kind of games, however only insofar as the result made the boy feel superior to Burtevertree, instead of a feeling of accomplishment at successfully building something. It was frustrating to Burtevertree but he persisted in getting the boy to play those games that involved at least some constructive activity along with the comparison between males.

23   TEALER TEACHING BY GAMES

Lorimorning's second child was also a male, this one clearly of Burtevertree's characteristics. Within months the older boy was trying to get the new boy to play games with him; and Burtevertree's task became one of teaching both to be constructive, and finally the older boy caught on to the idea of making himself look better than the littler one, by being better at building some kinds of things. Eventually Burtevertree was rewarded when he saw the older boy teaching the growing infant one of the constructive games; even if the purposes of the players were different, at least the same game was being played.

Game-playing had been almost an exclusively Town Leader type activity, even of the boys in their education, while Burtevertree grew up. As the Town Leaders were also the town teachers of the separated boys and girls, the obsession the Town Leaders had for playing games with each other, particularly formed as small teams pitted against each other, was an intrinsic part of their educational process. Every teaching was a game.

The older children were taught stylized group rituals that acted out both ways of human interacting but also at times imitated natural phenomena. A team of boys would learn to pretend to be a natural phenomena, like snow in the winter, taking on the qualities of snow falling, covering the ground, melting, becoming water. The boys who were closer to Town Leader genetics seemed to be better at this form of pretense, acting out natural phenomena in such a way that opposing teams and the onlookers would be able to picture the natural phenomena happening, even though it was physically only a team of other boys actively portraying the phenomenon like snowing happening.

There had been a standard set of such games taught to children growing up, involving all the natural phenomena and human interaction types. By acting out each kind of thing, each student became intimately connected with what was being taught. All knowledge thus involved some complex set of motions, particularly performed as small groups of students. This group involvement in all that was done, created an uncanny coordination within a team.

Yet it also provided a form of coercive behavior modification, the punishment of being isolated from all others. The intrinsic arrogant and brutal nature of the Town Leader genetics had to be early controlled, so when a boy exhibited the aggressive violent mode toward another boy, he would be punished by being put in an enclosure by himself, usually one that was on the edge of town where even the sound of other people would rarely be heard. To someone conditioned to only take action as part of a team, this isolation both turned off the aggression by having no one to aggress against, but also removed the sense of others being on a team leading to abuse another boy. It usually took only one or two stints at the isolation punishment to condition a boy to not quickly act out his arrogance and aggressive violent nature. This worked far better than physically harming the misbehaving boy, because abusing him even as corrective punishment effort, simply taught the boy to express more abusive behavior.

The aggressive nature thus was only expressible as a team, and was taught to be performed as part of a game. The Town Leader genetics thus tended to become best at participating in such games, and thus became more competent to become Town Leader candidates when they became adults.

History was taught similarly by the acting out of past human events. Opposing teams would act out historical events including fables, each team functioning as if just one person, thus the historical interaction of what had been just two people, would be performed by two teams. The various members of the teams would take on expression of particular qualities of the individual being portrayed, emphasizing stance or particular limb motions, or emotion or logical planning or cunning, each quality being emphasized by just a few among the team portraying the person. Thus the educational system taught that people had particular qualities and the combination of these qualities at any given moment of a person's doings, was known as the group of qualities expressing, not just as a single doing by the person.

If possible, other students would be used to express physical objects or natural phenomena, but stage props were allowed too. The boys who had less of the Tealer genetics, tended to utilize physical objects as stage props utilized in the games. A branch of a bush would represent a large tree, for example. Utilizing some qualities of the stage props to represent natural phenomena and physical objects, was easier for the non-Town-Leader genetic boys who preferred to have other boys of their team take on the physical properties of what would be stage props. Everything was anthropomorphized by the Tealer type boys, and as they grew up they became uncanny in their abilities to interact with real physical objects and inanimate objects, seemingly able to become them and even manipulate them from a distance at times, especially when a team of boys simultaneously portrayed the same object or event.

Thus in the many years of education of the boys, the Town Leader genetic expression boys became very competent at arranging events to seemingly just happen naturally. But they also were not very skilled at constructively dealing physically with real objects such as building things, so the non-Town-Leader types became specialized slaves that would do the actual building of homes, the crafting of tools, the constructors of measurement instruments, the physical creators of mining and smelting and casting of metals, the refinement of shaping of metal objects. They were the builders of homes, washing machines, electric motors and generators, wagons and trucks. Before the Town Leader genetics was introduced to the town folks, they were quite adept at building the things of a small scale industrialized way of life.

But now that the Town Leader males had invaded the town and taken control of it, and through proclaiming that all males be celibate - except the Town Leaders were exempt from that ruling - there were but few of the non-Town-Leader type males to perform the building and maintaining of homes and other items needed by the townspeople.

The town began to realize that something was being snuffed out as part of themselves with succeeding generations; the ability to manipulate events through team activity, was being greatly strengthened, but at the cost of the ability to make the things people needed to have to live and function. It became increasingly clear that the end point of this was to have the town become a breeder for more Town Leader menfolk, but that would slow and cease when the womenfolk could no longer take over the constructive tasks the their own original menfolk had been skilled at doing. When that point was reached, there was only one thing to happen: the army of Town Leader type men would have to invade and take over another town, to get the items needed for survival.

That had dimly been apparent to Burtevertree by the time he became an adult, one of the few men who were not much of the Town Leader genetics. He thus was valuable to the Town Leaders as a builder, a craftsman, a repairman, and it seemed there was an almost overwhelming need for him to be doing these things constantly.

To the Town Leaders, Burtevertree was a valuable useful thing, but one that became of zero value when it wanted to breed with a woman; all women were there only for the reproduction of the Tealer Town Leader men. The clever disposal of Burtevertree, just as was done to hundreds of men before him when they became resistant to the teachings of celibacy, was performed by just a team of two Town Leaders who were also skilled at driving a truck.

The town had to adapt to the loss of the two truck drivers and the truck, but also of the process of easily eliminating non-Tealer men who might procreate by one of the town's women. This would slow down the assimilation of the town as a breeding site for the town leader genetic males.

So the thirty primary Town Leaders held a special set of games, formed into five teams of six men each. the overall game posed the question of how to replace the function of the two Town Leaders and their truck, both in the fake repair service the two had performed, but also in the actual clever removal and disposal of the Non-Town-Leader genetic adult males when they would begin trying to court a woman. In the complex swirl of the thirty men acting out various aspects of the problem in their dance, as usual some would take on a solution being acted out; the various teams each would portray their solution as part of the complex performance, the portrayals that appeared to have greater potential to most perfectly fulfill the satisfaction of the posed question, became the way they solved the problem.

There were again a team of six men who utilized one of the remaining operational trucks, to gather up the harvest from the surrounding agriculture, and bring the food to the town's storage for the winter. They would carry out the abductions, but they would do it with three people on each disposal trip, making it harder for them to fail at the task. They did not know exactly what happened to cost them the first truck and pair of Town Leaders while they were on a task of disposing of a non-celibate male; and that two women had vanished about the same time, might have been part of it all too. So the use of three men to dispose of each single non-celibate male, ought to provide adequate strength both of physical prowess and cunning of teamwork conniving to overwhelm the target male.

The combined dance of the thirty prime Town Leaders finished, and as part of it, three of the members of one of the teams immediately left to get their truck, and already knew which of the males had recently been detected expressing non-celibate tendencies, interested in a woman.

Soon they had him bound and gagged, in the farm utility truck.

This was as had always been successful in the past by the prior two who performed that kind of task. However, they did not know the destination of the prior truck's disposal trips, but they knew which road to take. So off they drove, the three men ever busy playing a game amongst themselves that included getting the truck driven as well as planning what could be done to dispose of the abducted man in the back of the truck.

They drove and drove, looking for some obvious way to dispose of the man such that he would never be found. They paused at several odd looking places; they had never been so far from town. But there was just this one longer road trail through the terrain. Then they came to where the road veered off strangely; suddenly the terrain in front was vanishing; the few seconds it took for the team of three to reach a dance of agreement, also took the truck over the edge of the cliff.

24   TEALERS AND TRUCK AT BOTTOM

The loud clanging bang reverberated all around the canyon bottom, surprising the folks who were conducting a museum educational activity at the site of the wrecked seed ship. What could have caused that sound? Maybe another seed ship had just crashed. But as Burtevertree thought about the direction and apparent distance of the sound, he suspected it was caused by another truck going over the cliff. One of the lakeside town's couples accompanied Burtevertree and Lorimorning as they went to investigate, leaving the children to continue their education there by the other adult pairs.

The path to the cave tunnel entrance was well worn, but from there, it ran to the forest home of Lorimorning and Burtevertree's family. Along that path was the turnoff to the remains of the offshoot path that had been used when scavenging for truck parts for the electric system they used. This part of the path had overgrown and thus was slow going, but clearly different from the forestry to either side of the trail. Finally they arrived at the base of the cliff. The dismal scene of crumpled truck parts and human remains yet to be buried properly that had accumulated over the many prior decades was still there, but now a bit further away there was another truck and several more human remains, fresh ones, four of them. Three were of the physical characteristics of Tealers, and the fourth was not, and he also had been bound and gagged, but the Tealer men were not so constrained.

Lorimorning then again related the story of how she got down here, seeking what was going on with the abducted boyfriend of her girlfriend. Burtevertree filled in with his later urging the abandoned truck over the cliff so as to not have it there to reveal this site down here, now home to he and Lorimorning by then.

The new crumpled truck was many yards from the remains of the first truck, and Burtevertree suggested that it had been moving fairly fast when it went over the edge of the cliff; thinking about the road high above them on the plateau, it veered sharply at the cliff's edge and if a truck were to be traveling from the direction of the town, it would have gone right through the brush where the former boots and leather clothing items had been taken from the victims before tossing them over the cliff. A search did indeed find a scattering of leather clothing items, long weathered, now strewn about the base of the cliff. Burtevertree worried that not all the clothing items would have been knocked over the cliff, some might be still up there and now in plain sight for the next truck to perhaps find, and thus lead to discovery of this land down here, home of Burtevertree and Lorimorning with their children.

Yet the hole from the cave tunnel had been filled in to conceal its presence, and this also made it so it could not be used to go clear off the possible debris alongside of the road. Possibly the place could be reached by coming from the lake itself.

Lorimorning suggested that this may have been an initial effort to replace the original two men and truck that had been used for decades to dispose of non-celibate non-Tealer men. That there had been three of the Tealer men driving the truck, instead of the two that had done the task in the decades before, it indicated they thought there was a need for more strength to cope with a struggling victim. That they had driven right over the cliff, indicated that they were not familiar with the road.

She then suggested that unless the situation in town was involving a lot of non-celibate men, it would be many weeks before there would be another excursion down the road to dispose of non-celibate men. Thus they had some time to figure this out better. If they indeed did travel to the lake end of the cave tunnel, use a boat to reach access to the land, and then hike over to the road, find the cliff edge and finish tossing off any old leather items remaining up there, and then erase their tracks best possible on their way retracing their path to the lake, it would involve a lot of effort and risk of getting lost, or even seen by some of the Tealer kind cruising around in one of the remaining town trucks. It needed to be carefully planned out, and they probably had plenty of time to do it.

The couple that had come along from the lakeside town's educational museum activity, was impressed by the many kinds of remains here at the base of the cliff. They offered to return to help bury the remains of those who had perished here, as well as do some documentation of it all. This was part of history, even though not pleasant. And it did tie in with their history involving the abuses by the Tealer men of their town and finally the ousting of the Tealer men from the town; that they had not perished in the forest without women to reproduce themselves, but instead had become a parasite using another town to breed more of themselves apparently to then go raid more towns - it was part of the Tealer genetics to instinctively believe they were to be the only type of males to exist and thus was their heritage to eventually eliminate all other genetic type males.

The lakeside town had some data provided by the ones who had seeded this planet, a bit about history and types of people. The Tealer genetic type had long been with humanity and seemed to ever be stirring up violent conflicts; and on old Earth even differing groups of Tealers were endlessly at violent conflict with each other, each defending its reproductive base while attempting to eliminate men of the other groups while taking their women. Eventually success had been reached that had somewhat integrated the Tealer genetics in the general population, and the Tealer's type did have excellent useful qualities especially where team effort was needed to be at its peak so as to accomplish some types of tasks. But there always was the risk that the old urge to make themselves the sole reproducing males of a world, would crop up again. And indeed now this world apparently was infected with that phenomenon, and by simply banishing the Tealer men as a group, so as to end the endless mischief they did as members of the lakeside town folk, they had unwittingly loosed them in concentrated form upon an unsuspecting world. And they had essentially ruined Burtevertree and Lorimorning's town; and down here were the bones of decades of non-Tealer men who had been tossed over the cliff to perish in their vanishing from town.

Burtevertree ruefully looked at a patch of bones, his own family genetic kinsmen no doubt. That they had not really voluntarily left to go to a distant town where there were women for them, as the Tealers told the town folks, was just part of the clever deceit of the Tealer genetic type.

Part of the problem was that it would take Tealer approaches to be able to cope with the long term risk to civilization that seemed the end result of Tealer urges to conquer and eliminate any not of their kind. What would the Tealers do when they had conquered all the towns of the planet, and there were no more male types that could build the things a civilization needs for survival, he wondered. He thought back and had noticed some effort by the Tealers of his town to get the women to take over building homes and vehicles, but the women already had too much to do in farming, food preparation and providing the Tealers with more babies as fast as possible.

And now the town had lost two of its four trucks that had been still able to operate. It's resources were diminishing while the population was expanding; surely there would be a crossover point where the town could not sustain itself anymore. Quite likely the Tealers would try to get the post-menopausal women to figure out how to get some of the broken down trucks of the town to work again; maybe they would be able to get another serviceable truck or two going that way. But without resources to build new vehicles, the agricultural products eventually could not be gathered up at harvest time, thus not enough food through a winter. And it would not be the Tealers who would go hungry, Burtevertree was sure. But eventually the Tealers who constantly played their team games instead of being productive to the town's thriving, would become more than could be supported. The Tealers would then have to embark on another journey to assimilate another town; it was too likely that they would head back to the lakeside town, knowing where it was, and probably having a grudge to settle too.

Yet there were the other old roads, worn into the terrain generations ago; where did they lead? Maybe the Tealers would decide to use the remaining trucks and use them to find a different town, use the trucks to shuttle their Tealer army to near the other town. Even the two remaining trucks of the town could eventually transport all the Tealers over to a camp where they could proceed with their tactics, probably first being friendly, then setting themselves up to be teachers and leaders of the town a few at a time. Eventually it would become a copy of Burtevertree's town. The existence of the Tealers seemed an almost overwhelming problem to Burtevertree, as he struggled to enable life here.

He remembered the Tealers even as they grew up. They did not seem a bad sort, and they seemed to endlessly have games to play competing against each other as teams, and Burtevertree had at times tried to join in so as to have some of the great fun too. But each time he tried joining in, the Tealers accepted him but then he found they simply were too clever and too many of them on all sides for him to be successful at anything he tried to do in the game-playing; and sometimes when a deliberate violation of the game playing was done by one of the teams of Tealers, the blame and punishment was always directed at Burtevertree even though he had seen the Tealers do the wrong thing themselves. Eventually Burtevertree would give up again, while the Tealers just kept on their endless sports ever busy in a swirl of Tealers clearly stimulated into happy feelings by their vigorous gaming.

25   THE MISSING NUTRIENT

Burtevertree finally had gotten the message, that his lot was to not have the fun of the team games, but instead was to find whatever happiness there was in building and repairing things for the town's folks, including for the Tealers. He thought that surely the Tealers could use their teamwork to build things quite well, but so far, they did not seem to be doing that. And any efforts to get Tealers to do something, was considered an effort to control the Tealers, and that was not permitted; and the penalties were abusive and nearly instant, as a team of Tealers would turn on the unfortunate non-tealer who had been perceived as trying to give orders to the Tealers.

Still, the Tealers might shift to using their endless teamwork sport type activity to build things they needed, once they realized there were no other kinds of people left anymore to do that kind of task. Surely all they would have to do is make up games about building things, and then play the games and the homes and vehicles would get built in the fun and games.

Yet, how much more ruination would they do to other people, before that happened. If the Tealers got down here in the valley, there would be no place anymore to do agriculture and home-building, there would be no way for Burtevertree and his family to survive as the Tealer teams bounced around sporting all over the valley, leaving nothing alive in their wake.

He still did not want to do any harm to the Tealers; causing harm was a Tealer kind of response. Burtevertree was a builder, and survival of his family would have to depend on that kind of activity. Still, despite Lorimorning's first child being a Tealer, there was some acceptance by the lakeside people; and their mode of way of life, always as male-female pairs, seemed the same as Burtevertree chose to have life too. If it were not for their Tealer type firstborn, they would have eventually been able to join in with the lakeside town's folks, most likely. And he would not abandon their older son, Tealer type or not. In fact, the instincts of the older boy had been helpful at times, providing a bit of coordination when all had to pitch in to get a particular complex task done.

One of those tasks had been when there was a need to lift the remains of the crashed seed ship up to the level of the forest floor, and support it up there so that the underside could be cleaned off and restored as much as possible, to learn more about its mode of propulsion. The Tealer boy had stirred up a game fun attitude among the tired workers digging around and under the crashed vehicle, and soon they were all heave-ho back and forth, rocking the shell of the vehicle, while also working its way up the side of the dug out area. Once the diggers all figured out what was going on, they expanded on using tools to improve the movement process, and within two days the vehicle was entirely up on level ground, and even set up on pedestals made of cliff face rock shards.

The lakeside town's more scientifically inclined pairs of folks were finally able to better evaluate the crashed vehicle. It was made of an outer shell of foamed ceramic-nickel-iron blend material, very strong and light weight. The horizontally circular shaped outer shell supported a pair of large rings just inside the hull, and these rings appeared to be electromagnetically inductive to an electric motor that drove an airscrew at the back of the vehicle. Maybe there had been one in the front too, but would have been destroyed if so. Apparently the pair of large rings must have been spinning at a high rate of speed, and the energy was slowly inductively taken off to drive the airscrew. But what had made the pair of rings spin around in the first place?

That the vehicle had crashed just below the Humming-Wire, seemed to suggest that maybe the vehicle was intending to get energy from the Humming-Wire's high velocity, to speed up the rings inside the vehicle; and maybe the seed ship had not been quite able to reach the Humming Wire before it lost too much energy to propel itself, and had bumped into the face of the cliff, and down it came.

If so, there would have to be some structure in the vehicle that enabled it to couple energy from the Humming-Wire into its internal spinning rings. So finally they found a section of the vehicle's shell that would lift to expose the pair of spinning rings; they must then have electromagnetically contacted the Humming Wire to replenish their energy. So it seemed that the seed ship would probably have periodically come over to the tower atop the cliff, replenish its spin energy from the humming-wire, then head off to dump more canisters of self-reproducing biosystem starts. The seed ship would have needed to be able to travel a long ways from here to do so.

Were there any more of the towers with humming wires located elsewhere on the planet, on which the seed ships could regain energy for their activities? Or was there only one such power source, and maybe only this one seed ship ever to be here?

Once the seedship was cleaned off and detailed examination of it was ongoing by the scientists of the lakeside town, they found meaning for some of the appendages of the vehicle. There was a tube and valve leading from inside the vehicle that opened into the top of the vehicle; electrolysis of water apparently separated one of water's molecules that then were exited to the spout on top of the vehicle, while the other gas was released to the interior of the vehicle, at least part of it. That would mean oxygen for the interior, and that left the hydrogen to be put through the spout and valve on top of the vehicle. Careful examination of the upper surface of the pancake-shaped vehicle, showed there were remains of what had been a film that ringed the outer edge of the vehicle's top; a more careful search of the dirt that had been dug away from the top of the vehicle, resulted in finding patches of a very thin fabric, apparently a monomolecular-thickness fabric, a carbon-based film of great strength. Thus it was concluded that a huge hydrogen-filled bag on top of the vehicle was what supported the weight of the vehicle by displacing atmosphere of higher density. Samples of this bag material were eagerly taken back to the labs in town; if they could duplicate it, there would be many uses.

Meantime the biologists were exploring their principle of balance in biological systems. This balance was evident in the biodiversity of the seeded biology of the terrain. What they were worried about, were some essential components of the biosystem not seeded, due to the loss of the seedship here? Had the canisters contained something that would be necessary for survival in the long term?

Lorimorning pointed out that they had found one canister which they had opened, to not be a rotted mess, but instead contained viable seeds, and she was growing some of the plants in her garden. The plant did not seem to be anywhere else in the valley, nor of the agriculture of her town of origin either. It produced a small round seed that seemed quite nutritious. And she had found that it seemed to contain some component that when fed to her older son, his Tealer type obnoxiousness seemed to fade away. But the boy apparently needed to have some of that plant food each day, to continue to behave better.

When she told the lakeside town's folks about this, there was some excitement about it and a request to make trade for some of the seeds of that plant. Their biosystem theorists had gotten the idea that maybe the Tealers were a product of an unbalanced biosystem, and that maybe it was the lack of some chemical made by this very plant, had been missing from the environment, and thus led to the Tealers going run-amok. Two of the lakeside couples came to observe Lorimorning's oldest son, Tealer that he clearly was, as he behaved both without any of the new plant food for several days, then how he behaved while resuming having some of the seeds of that plant in his diet each day. They too concluded that his behavior was significantly different when the added food was part of his diet. It was a repeatable phenomenon. The Tealer boy did not lose his capability for teamwork, but he did seem to cease having the craving to outdo others at any cost, whether by deception or by violence; he instead chose to simply be more cooperative with others and seemed to find enjoyment in being that way instead of by being dominant through mischief.

The town's sociobiologists were very interested in all this, and suggested that maybe the seeds were intended from the beginning to be a moderator for the Tealer type of person, enabling them to be cooperatively integrated into human society as a whole. Thus the Tealer problem was seen as perhaps merely an unbalanced biosystem effect.

They put the older boy through several more cycles of doing without the new seed food for long enough to have him start to be aggressive against others; then adding in a little of the seed nutrition into his diet, to see how much of it was needed to make him better integrate into their social system. Lorimorning agreed to only those few cycles of research on her older son, then she insisted that he have a plentiful supply of the seed in his daily meals from now on. Besides, she had found that having the new grain as part of her own and Burtevertree's daily meals, they seemed less stressed and distracted in their daily work. Best of all, they could think a bit more clearly. And Burtevertree felt that they indeed had huge problems to resolve.

26   RESCUING TEALER CAPTIVES

It was beginning to occur to Burtevertree that the new seed of the plant grown from the canister from the wreck of the seedship, might be a tool for dealing with the probability of being overrun by the Tealers. He contemplated the possible effects if the seed were somehow scattered among the other seeds in his former town's farms. But he decided that any Tealers who had eaten the new seeds for awhile and thus if they too became better mannered, that the other Tealers would see the easygoing Tealers as inferior, due to their otherwise obsessive endless testing of who was better than whom in the maintaining of their hierarchy. Those who became milder mannered would thus be cast down to the bottom of the social structure. The supreme thirty Tealers ruling the town would probably identify the new odd-looking grain as being something that caused them to not function triumphantly as they had before, and forbid its agriculture.

Besides, he did not see a way to deliver the seed to the agricultural fields of the town now controlled by the ever-watchful uncanny Tealers. It had been about a two-hour ride in the truck to get here from town; it would be a much longer walk back. If he was spotted by the Tealers, surely he would not live much longer. Maybe if Lorimorning were to do the seed delivery to the agricultural fields, as the Tealers were likely to just take her back into their women group reproductive pool; they had not known how she had vanished, anyway. But neither she nor Burtevertree were willing for that to happen. Yet at this point, it seemed the first thing that they had found that might be able to resolve the huge problem of coping with the Tealers, if it could be correctly utilized. Lorimorning suggested with a small smile that they might invite the Tealers over for dinner.

The lakeside town's folks took this idea a bit further, making a project to grow and store as much of the new seed as possible, for some possible use if invaded by the Tealers. It seemed perhaps a way to deal with the problem of probable invasion by the tealers, the other way being for all the men to leave town, and the Tealers take over all the women and all the vehicles and resources made by the townsfolk.

So they immediately integrated the new seed into their daily diet, every meal; it did seem to reduce their stress level and increase their comprehension of things, their competency generally increasing. And if the Tealers were to come invade here and partake of meals from the town's food supply, they would get the new nutritional ingredient too, like it or not.

The lakeside townsfolk were highly creative and productive, ever functioning as male-female pairs. Their scientists blended with their engineers who blended with those who built things who blended with the larger population that utilized those products. It was a system of knowledge flow in both directions, ever improving the products and enabling new things to be created.

They had concentrated on reproducing the fabric that had been found atop the seedship, finding it to be a series of overlapping layers of carbon atoms such that there was no way for the tiny hydrogen molecules to pass through. Then they had made bags of the material, used electrolysis of water to fill the bags with hydrogen, and had a couple of the tethered bags straining at their tethers lashed to the ground in town. They tested putting a torch against one of the bags and found the bag merely got taught due to warming expansion of the hydrogen gas inside, but neither ripped the strong bag nor ignited the hydrogen, there being no way for oxygen to get in nor for hydrogen to get out into the air. Soon the engineering and manufacturing experts were busy building a floating vehicle that used electrolysis to add hydrogen to a supportive bag and then if the load lightened, to release some of the hydrogen, so as to maintain neutral buoyancy overall. It seemed to be part of what had supported the seed ship while traveling around delivering its biological products.

They also made a pair of contra-rotating rings spinning around a common center, each supported by magnetic bearings, in imitation of the seedship. There even was talk of putting a large hydrogen bag back atop the seedship, and seeing if they could lift it up and evaluate how it coupled its circular rings to the Humming Wire. But that seemed a one-time opportunity thing and they needed to learn a lot more before they tried such a thing. Besides, they did not know how to control the seed ship even if they could lift it and get its rings to spin again. Meanwhile their own pair of spinning rings was clearly useful for storing energy and they got it to supply some nighttime lighting to their town.

The closest they got to imitating the seedship's probable functional mode, was to lift one of the small spinning ring energy storage pairs up as supported by a hydrogen filled bag, all tethered to the ground. They set up an incandescent light to be powered by drawing energy from the spinning ring, and at night, the thing lifted into the night sky while glowing brightly, spread some light all over the town for awhile until the energy was too far spun down to keep the lamp lit. Still it was an interesting experiment.

Burtevertree asked how long a tether could they make for a hydrogen filled floating bag; if they used the same basic material for the tether as the bag, with many redundant strands, they were confident that it could be made to be very long. And a month later, they had him strapped below a hydrogen bag, with a valve in hand to enable easy lowering of himself if the experiment got out of control, and up he went on the tether, payed out from a reel on the ground. However, as the apparent size of people and things on the ground got a lot smaller, he also found it got a lot colder, and a bit hard to breathe, so he let some hydrogen out until it was apparent he was now going back down.

They next used two tethers, one at each end of the valley, and lifted him by the dual-tethered hydrogen bag, initially going up at one end of the sunken valley, and traveled along high above the treetops of the forest below, to again set down at the other end of the valley, at the other reel. That was an easy way to travel the twelve kilometers across the sunken canyon. Could it be adapted to be used to spread seed all over the agricultural land of the Tealer's conquered town? Although they did not see how to get such apparatus installed over there, they at least developed the technology to do it.

Meanwhile they also seeded all their agricultural land so that some of the new seed would be in any harvest from their land; it was very nutritious to themselves too. And if the Tealer army invaded and ate food from the town, hopefully it would balance them like it had balanced Lorimorning's Tealer-fathered son. Would the nutrition have the same effect on an adult male Tealer such as in the prime ruler thirty Tealer men who ruled the town? Or had their developed ways become too ingrained to change enough to enable them to become a functional part of human society. No one was willing to go try to capture a full-grown Tealer over at the town, to do the experiment, understandably.

Burtevertree predicted that by this time, more boys would have matured to the point of resenting the celibacy rules imposed on the non-pure-Tealer young men, and that the thirty leaders of the town would choose to risk losing another of their farm trucks rather than endure the problem of the young men being romantic with the women of the town. Therefore it was likely that it would not be much longer before another truck would be coming down the road, maybe carrying more than one captive young man for disposal. He did not want to be having to clean up the mess made if they too went over the cliff to smash down here.

So the lakeside town's manufacturers made a more advanced tethered floating vehicle, which carried both Burtevertree and Lorimorning, and positioned them above the road each day during the hours typical of the disposal journeys by the Tealers in the past. The two were settled in fairly comfortably in the cabin slung under the the balloon, and was positioned about a mile ahead of the place where the road veered away from the cliff's edge. The airship was tethered where it could see a truck coming down the road, yet not be likely to be seen themselves, up in the air and hidden by forest foliage.

They carried two bags of dark mud, and when indeed a truck was coming down the road, they dropped the mud bags to splash all over the windshield of the truck, causing it to have to stop, long before reaching a dangerously near part of the cliff. They then lowered the airship by retracting on the tether, then Lorimorning got out and unbound all three bound and gagged young men in back of the farm truck. Meantime, Burtevertree disabled the truck from being able to be restarted, while one of the Tealers was trying to wipe off the sticky mud from the windshield, not having much success without any water for rinsing it off he was getting quite frustrated. Another Tealer got out of the truck to help him wipe the window.

Lorimorning got the freed captives to run into the forest, and in a moment Burtevertree and Lorimorning were reeling out the tether to climb high over the vehicle again.

Several couples from the lakeside town were stationed in the area, hiding in the forest, and hurried to encounter the freed captives. The young men had figured out that they probably would not survive the trip, that they were not being taken to some distant town where there were plenty of women for them; and so they were eagerly accepting the offer to help, by the pairs of folks from the lakeside town, clearly not Tealers, although were strangers. They all withdrew from the vicinity of the truck; but they did see that there were four of the Tealer men inside the front of the truck, to make sure they could handle any emergency posed by the three captives while they were being eliminated.

Another couple from the lakeside town went up in another tethered airship, far enough away for safety, but where they could watch the Tealers as they coped with their unexpected situation. As typically, they endlessly bounced around as if playing a ball game, finally getting the window clean enough to be able to drive down the road; but then they discovered that the vehicle would no longer run. And then they discovered that no one was in the back of the farm truck either. As night fell, the four Tealers got back into the front of the truck, sitting in the middle of the road. They continued to try to start the vehicle, but none of them had any aptitude for fixing anything when it no longer worked normally.

27   SIX MORE TEALERS

By the next morning, the four Tealers were clearly hungry and were scavenging in the forest nearby, finding berries and fruit. By the second day the four had traveled quite a ways from the truck to find more of the fairly scarce edibles; and while they were gone from the truck, Burtevertree and Lorimorning dropped down in the airship, and set a container of nicely prepared food on the seat of the truck; it was the kind of food accustomed by the dominant Tealers, except this time it was laced with a heavy helping of the new grain.

Then they raised up high again in the tethered airship, pulled over to the side to be hidden by the trees in the opposite direction to where the Tealers had gone to hunt for food. And later that day, the Tealer team was bouncing down the road back to the truck, to spend the night; the woods was no safe appearing place to them. Finding the container of food on the seat of the truck, they eagerly ate it, and all was quiet as night fell.

Lorimorning told the lakeside town folk that they now had four samples of Tealers on which to test the new food's effect, and had already been given some of the food, although was not known if all of them ate of it. Uncertain of how to handle the situation, several of the town couples observed the truck from a safe distance; sure enough, apparently the dominant Tealer of the group had eaten all the food gathered by the other three Tealers from the edibles in the forest; so those three ate the food offering left by Lorimorning on the truck seat; now this morning, one

Tealer was out and appeared a bit upset because the other three Tealers were being slow to get going to forage in the forest this morning. But they got going, still doing the endless teamwork bouncing around playing a game of ball while they headed down the forest road to where they left off gathering edibles the previous two days. But there was much less food to forage within walking distance to the truck this time, and so when they got back to the truck that evening, the freshly cooked delicious smelling container of food was eagerly eaten by all four men.

The next morning the men mostly milled around the truck, not so coordinated nor often tossing a ball back and forth between themselves to keep up the endless teamwork. They seemed mostly trying to figure out where the food was coming from. And thus no new supply of food appeared for their dinner. Finally as dusk was starting, five of the couples from the lakeside town came out of the forest, bringing a container of food for the Tealers. The townsfolk had decided that five couples would represent more males than were Tealers in the situation; and all being couples, that each man was teamed with a helpful woman, was intended to communicate that mode of relationship.

The group of five lakeside townsfolk stopped about 30 feet from the truck-full of Tealers who were watching them approach. Setting down two containers of aromatic cooked food, and a jug of water, the five couples then backed down the road a ways then faded into the forest, helped by the dimming light of dusk. The townsfolk gone only a few minutes, one of the Tealers got out of the truck, and brought back one of the containers; soon the other container had also been taken into the truck by the Tealers.

The experiment seemed to be working at least a little bit. That one Tealer had gotten out by himself either voluntarily or by coercion by the leader of the team, was just not a normal thing to happen; the Tealers always did things as a team together. Always before, they would have gotten out of the truck together and would have been tossing a ball or other object back and forth between them as they went down the road to investigate the food containers.

A week later the four Tealers had been settled into a hastily made house at the edge of the road, and seemed content to be served daily with fresh food and water; they still were locked in there while the food and drink was being placed outside, then the door unlocked and the lakeside folks hurried away into the forest. During one of these times of the Tealers being locked in, Burtevertree and Lorimorning went to the farm truck, she finished washing the mud off the windshield while he repaired the truck so it would start; they then drove it half a mile away and hid it in the foliage beside the road, before they returned to their home; Burtevertree had again disabled the vehicle, just to make sure it stayed there.

Burtevertree wondered what the ruling thirty Tealers would pick as their next strategy. He knew he was no match for their master strategists, but he knew they now had only one running farm truck left. And it was getting to be close to harvest time; the remaining truck would be greatly needed to bring in the harvest for survival through the coming winter. He guessed that there would be no further trucks coming this way for a long time.

He was wrong. Only two weeks later, the remaining farm truck came down the road, this time with six of the Tealers inside, four in front and two more in back with the three bound and gagged young men who had apparently chosen to cease to be celibate any more. And this time there was no welcoming committee to dump mud on a windshield; but the truck was seen coming down the road from kilometers away, by the town lookout who was now daily stationed high in a tethered airship. They managed to get two couples to the side of the road by the time the truck got near the sharp bend in the road, and they hurled bags of mud at the truck; one bag got part of the windshield and the other bag went into the open side window and splattered all over the driver. This got the truck stopped, but almost immediately the six Tealers were out bouncing around the truck, ready for any game to win over whoever had stopped them. They gave no chance to release their captives, nor to disable the truck.

By this time, Burtevertree and Lorimorning had arrived

overhead in the airship, unnoticed by the Tealers who had glimpsed the mud-throwers from the forest. Two of the Tealers had brought bows and arrows, and now held them at the ready; they were determined to resolve the losses of the other trucks. It was mid-morning and not easy to fade into the forest; but as always, the Tealers only went as a group, both uncannily stalking their victim while also they were bouncing around with the ballgame they endlessly played together, which was integrated into their team activity. So the group of six Tealers ran after one of the lakeside town couples, who tried to escape into the forest but were caught by the Tealers. Meanwhile the airship dropped down and Burtevertree disabled the truck while Lorimorning freed the captives and urged them to run and hide in the forest as fast as possible. The airship rose and backed a bit out of sight in the trees nearby. Soon the bouncing bunch of Tealers returned to the truck, dragging the woman of the couple they had chased down.

This did not look good to the airship pair, as the townsfolk never went anywhere without each other. So they urged the airship out over above where there had apparently been a struggle in the edge of the forest; there they found the man, several arrows in him, but still alive. The airship could only carry two people, so Burtevertree stayed on the ground, while Lorimorning flew the airship over to where she knew some of the townsfolk were located, and gave them the injured man; then she hurried back to get Burtevertree. Back in the air, they discovered that they had been spotted by the Tealers, and an arrow pierced the bottom of their cabin, as they tugged on one of the tethers while also releasing the other tether; up they went fast and off to the side. But they were not out of sight of the enraged Tealer team, who fruitlessly expended the rest of their arrows trying to reach the airship.

The remaining tether was anchored down in the bottom of the sunken canyon; the Tealers soon encountered the edge of the cliffs. The airship stayed in place, now far above the tether place in the bottom of the canyon. After a few minutes the Tealers headed back to their truck, only to find their captives gone, and the truck would not start. But this bunch of Tealers seemed far more coordinated than the previous bunch; although the more Tealers in a team, the better they seemed to function as if one mind. And these were as determined as any Tealer; Lorimorning said she recognized several of them; they were among the thirty dominant ruler Tealers of the town. Maybe even one of them was the father of her first son; which of the dominant thirty Tealers would not be known by even them. But clearly this was going to be a tougher bunch of Tealers.

Everybody got as far away as they could, from the bunch of Tealers who had gathered around the truck again, acting calmly and with deliberation while bouncing the ball amongst themselves. However, when the truck would not run, they did not stay there in the truck, but immediately started to forage in the forest. Then they returned, still a team, and got out some containers of food and water they had brought along. Master strategists, these were better prepared for this trip's expected difficulties. They still had the woman of the lakeside couple, and bound and gagged her in the back of the truck, and four of the Tealers stayed in there with her, while the other two spent the night in the front cab of the truck. In the morning, they continued to feed from both the edibles gathered from the forest, but also from the provisions they had brought along; although it looked like they had only prepared for a day's worth of nutrition on this adventure.

Lorimorning especially felt sorry for the captive woman, but thought that the Tealers would not badly harm her, considering her as breeding material. The condition of her husband was unknown, but he would be tended by the experts in the lakeside town; yet he had been badly injured by three arrows shot into him, left for dead. The Tealers had come to do battle with whoever was interfering with their non-celibate men's disposal process, and it appeared that this couple was involved. Enraged by the missing men captives and by the problem of not getting the truck running again, they vented their rage on the woman, demanding she tell them what was going on. They could be heard yelling into the night, until the battery in the truck no longer could keep the truck's lights going.

The next morning, there was no one bringing food for the Tealers this time. The Tealers got out of the truck and headed as a group, bouncing down the road to find new forage, but stayed in sight of the truck where their bound captive was tied. Burtevertree and Lorimorning watched from their airship just above the forest canopy, having re-established the second tether overnight. They were not willing to risk any more arrows being shot at them; besides, they did not know if the hydrogen bag would survive a hit by an arrow. And the team of Tealers remained at a distance from the truck such that their strong legs would carry them back within moments. However, the foraging was slim, already having been picked over the day before; so they went further down the road. Then a bit further, occasionally coming back enough so one of them could look at the truck. Then he would vanish into the forest.

28   THE FOURTH TEALER TRUCK

It looked too much like a setup to Burtevertree, but Lorimorning said they had to rescue the woman as quickly as possible. Burtevertree suspected that the Tealers had stealthily returned to near the truck as they hid in the forest. How badly hurt was the woman, was an unknown; she made no sound, lying bound in the bottom of the back of the farm utility truck.

Then suddenly from above the forest, the lookout in the high airship was over the forest near the truck, was hurling objects into the forest below, then suddenly the team of Tealers sprouted out of the forest and hurled stones back at the airship; Burtevertree counted all six Tealers, so he dropped off the airship, quickly repaired the truck, but its battery was dead and so would not start. He then got into the back of the truck and found the woman very securely tied down; it would take a long time to free her; Lorimorning demanded he get back into the airship and they headed away before the team of Tealers returned to the truck.

The next morning, the Tealer team again headed out down the road, two of them carrying the bound up woman, who now appeared too injured to walk. The muscular Tealers had no problem carrying her, each of two men using only one arm to hold her as they jogged down the road. Apparently abandoning the truck, they soon were seen to have a pattern of rapidly moving down the road back toward town, then pausing to go into the forest to gather whatever handy edibles were to be found, then munch them as they continued on down the road toward home.

To Burtevertree it looked like a workable strategy; they were likely to be able to get back to town that way in a couple of days. They were physically powerful men, long fed the best food of the town, and probably could get to town on a run even without stopping for the forest's edibles that were handy. The Tealers were out of range of the tethered airship already.

They took the airship to get firewood from their home, and Burtevertree used it to get the small starter external combustion engine started on the truck, then letting the engine recharge its battery for awhile. He then drove the truck several miles down the road, past the sharp curve in the road, resisting the urge to run it off the cliff too. He found a place to hide the truck at the edge of the road; he had never been this far down the road, far past the cliff where most of the action had occurred. He carefully returned along the edge of the forest; and spotted by Lorimorning, was picked up in the airship. Yes, he had disabled the truck again although now its battery had some charge in it, so it could be started again with a bit of repair to the vehicle done first.

The next day the lakeside town folk met with Burtevertree and Lorimorning to discuss the situation. They now had two farm trucks that could be gotten to run again, and they had four mellowed out Tealer men in a restrained housing situation, well-fed with the new grain; they seemed to be behaving themselves. The other part was that there were six top Tealers headed back to town, bringing along a lakeside town couple's woman, and her husband was struggling to live, with arrows freshly removed from him, as he was cared for by the town's doctor, who had never dealt with such injuries before.

The Tealer leaders now knew where the action was happening, and knew of the airships. If that data got to the larger group

Tealer leaders, it could be devastating as the Tealers would use that in their uncanny strategies.

Finally Burtevertree told Lorimorning to quickly take him back to the freshly hidden truck, and leave him there, with only a few tools. Soon, he was on the road, driving the farm truck toward where the Tealers were jogging down the road. As he approached them from behind, he honked the horn and stopped. Stepping outside the truck, he shouted that he would trade the truck for the woman.

The Tealers ball-bounced around for a few moments, in their way of deciding things. Then they called to Burtevertree to bring the truck there and they would give him the woman. Burtevertree said no, one of them bring the woman over near the truck; they did so, dropping the unconscious and bound woman on the road. The Tealer returned to the group as they continued their ever in motion ball playing amongst themselves even in this situation. Burtevertree flipped the fuel line over to the small emergency tank, then got out and picked up the limp form of the woman, and started trudging down the road carrying her; he looked back to see if the Tealers were going to attack him, but they instead got into the truck, and headed off down the road toward town; they had precious data that would soon enable them to take over the situation.

Burtevertree was tired of carrying the limp woman by the time Lorimorning got the airship over to pick her up and carry her to safety; then soon she was back to get him. They rose as high as their tethers would allow, and were able to see that the truck was again stopped in the road a few miles away, the fuel in the emergency tank had run dry.

The next day, word from the lakeside town's folks was that the injured husband and wife were still alive but their long term fate was unknown; the woman had several broken bones and many bruises. At least both were conscious and cared for by the doctor; they now close to each other again. Burtevertree sulked, feeling this was all his fault, getting the lakeside folks involved, and trying to reform the Tealer men by means of the nutritional supplement. He thought the Tealers ought to be exterminated, like the lakeside folks had tried to do originally; they were incorrigible. Yet Burtevertree deeply cared for Lorimorning's first son, a Tealer too; the boy seemed quite well behaved, now that he had the missing nutrient in his diet. The captive Tealer men seemed to have become more calm, still playing their ballgame together, but not all the time anymore.

It took Burtevertree half a day to reach the truck on foot; arriving in sight of the truck, he watched until fairly sure the team had resumed the jogging toward town. Arriving at the truck, again looking around for possible attackers, he flipped the fuel valve toward the main fuel tank, cranked the engine; he turned the truck around and headed back down the road as fast as the truck would go.

But here were no attackers jumping out of the forest; powerful as the Tealer men were, they were even smarter and more clever than that. He got the truck back hidden where it had been, then suddenly realized the truck had felt a bit heavy as he drove it back; he had not taken the time to check in the back of the truck. The engine was still running, so he carefully backed the truck so that the back of it hung over the side of the canyon cliff, then turned the engine off, again switching over to the now empty spare tank, just in case. He opened the door, got out of the truck and ran; as he had stepped to the ground he noticed that the truck was briefly moving up and down; glancing at the back of the truck, he saw that both back doors were swung open; Tealer men could be soon climbing over the top of the truck to get on the ground to chase him, so he ran down the road a few hundred feet then into the forest briefly then back onto the road where he could move faster, now out of sight of the truck.

Lorimorning found him and soon they were high in the airship; Burtevertree asked her to fly it over to where they could see into the back of the truck as well as see any lurking Tealers around the truck at this time. No Tealers near the truck; its back doors were swung wide open, however; maneuvering around a bit, they verified there were no Tealers inside. Maybe he was imagining things, fearing that the cunning Tealers had hidden in the back of the truck, to ride inside to find out where it would be hidden, and to then assault him.

He was ready to call it a day's work done; he could come back tomorrow to hide the truck. But Lorimorning first wanted to lower down to the bottom of the cliff; she suspected that it could be that the Tealer team had indeed hidden in the back of the truck and then had come bouncing out the back of the truck as a unified team instead of looking then climbing to the top of the truck, as soon as they heard the engine being turned off. And yes, there they were, crumpled together at the bottom of the cliff. She said they could return in a few days to see if any on top had survived the fall by being cushioned by the ones on the bottom, like had saved her life; but right now she did not want to risk one of the Tealers surprising them. In a few days they could return through the forest bringing some of the lakeside folks to help them; for now, it was time for them to have a well earned rest.

On the way back home, Burtevertree was still planing what to do next; he wanted to see if the lakeside engineers could make a fully free-moving airship, not dependent on tether combinations to move it around; he wanted to go spread the seeds of the new plant all over the agricultural area of their former town. But Lorimorning just said that with no farm trucks at all, little would get harvested, and through the winter people would have to forage on the unharvested crop still in the field; the Tealers would have no doubt figured this out and would be involved with some other of their clever schemes. Most likely they would plot to attack the lakeside town to get food before winter struck, she predicted.

29   A FREE-FLYING AIRSHIP

It was clear to Burtevertree that at least one of the farm utility trucks had to be returned to the town, to enable their survival through winter. That the ruling Tealers might instead choose to use the truck to transport an army to striking distance of some neighboring town, instead of using it to harvest food for the winter survival of their town, was a risk that would have to be taken. As to how to deliver at least one of the farm utility trucks to the town, ready to be useful to the Tealers yet without getting caught delivering it, was yet to be determined.

The lakeside town's engineers said that they could not fully duplicate the energy storage rings that had been used on the seed ship, since they could not make the stronger permanent magnets with their existing materials and technologies. But maybe they could make a more conventional wheel device consisting of a dual coaxial contra-rotating central bearing mechanism, and explore that a bit. They would attempt to build a free-flying vehicle, with a harness for a flyer under a box containing the pair of spinning wheels, underslung below a partially inflated hydrogen gas bag, that could be transported in the back of a utility farm truck.

The engineers and craftsworkers of the little town worked as fast as possible, with a rough design; How well it would work in practice was a big unknown, as Burtevertree was going to have to make the first test flight in a real truck delivery.

And so Burtevertree found himself driving the second of the two farm utility trucks back down the road toward his town of origin early one morning; it was chilly and clear and a couple of hours before dawn. He arrived at the edge of town at first light; he picked a place to park the truck that would be seen as soon as people began to head for the fields to work. He pulled the untested flying machine out of the back of the utility truck, down a ramp to the ground, the gyroscopic action of the wheels that had been spun up before heading to town, making the move a bit awkward; but then it was on the ground. Looking around, he saw no one outside yet, was still too chilly to go work, and for him too although he was dressed as warmly as possible. He attached one arm and one leg to the under-straps, then opened the valve to release some compressed hydrogen into the bag on top of the vehicle; as soon as it had inflated enough to drag him free of the ground, he closed the valve, and with some struggle got his other arm and leg secured to the underside of the contraption. Then a bit more hydrogen and up he went.

The air was still, no breeze, so at this point he was about 50 feet above the utility truck when he noticed that he had left the truck's small running headlamp still turned on. It would eventually deplete the battery if no one either turned it off or else restarted the engine of the truck. Well, he only had this one chance to get away; he tested engaging the air screw shaft to the edge of the contra-rotating pair of wheels, and it began to move him along; shifting a rudder in the air screw's airflow, got him pointed back the way he came. As he passed over a corner of the agricultural fields, he threw out a handful of the new type seeds, hoping that they would survive and then thrive in the spring. It was now daylight enough to see the road, and he began a fairly slow travel along the highway, at a walk's pace, however.

An hour later, he found himself floating above the road, motionless; the energy storage wheels no longer providing any energy. He disconnected the coupling to the wheels, and began to crank on the airscrew by hand; he began to move again. But in the next 15 minutes, he had moved no further than he could have moved on foot, and he was tired of cranking. He headed over to the nearest taller tree that looked a bit recognizable beside the road, and let enough hydrogen out of the gas bag to drop to the ground, deflating the bag until it barely supported the weight of the vehicle without him attached; he quickly tied the vehicle to the tree, hidden down in the bushes. Then he headed down the road on foot, keeping to the side so he could try to hide in the roadside brush if the truck had been sent to grab him.

He estimated that he had traveled by air about 60 of the 100 miles needed to go to get back home. Forty more miles to go. He had covered about 25 miles of that by nightfall; he had no flashlight so he hid in the roadside brush in the last light. He had eaten one of the meals that Lorimorning had sent with him for the trip, not knowing if he would need them or not; he saved the second meal for breakfast in the morning, He shielded himself as much as possible from the night's cold, waited out the night.

Dawn's light was well ongoing by the time he woke up; stiffly he stretched, then got out the snacks and small container of water. Then looking carefully as possible he got back to the side of the road; listened, no sound of any pursuit at the moment. Resuming his walk down the road, the effort warmed him up a bit, increasing his speed a bit. He adopted an easy pace, a rhythmic lope that seemed one he could maintain endlessly. It was again nightfall when he recognized the sharp turn of the road that was near his home, but there was no way to get down into the canyon. He was exhausted and hungry; and just before he headed into the bushes to hide for the night, he saw a flashlight shining around from something suspended out over the canyon; he called out, and in fifteen minutes he was in the tethered airship with Lorimorning, as she winched the tethers to land them at their home.

Midday the next day, he and Lorimorning were in the remaining utility truck, headed down the road to retrieve the experimental airship. They had decided that if the town Tealers had not chosen to go chase down whoever brought the truck back, minus the Tealers that had left in it, then the Tealers would probably either be using the truck to start the harvest, or else be preparing to move their army to attack the lakeside town; either way it would be days until the truck would be headed this way. They needed to make their retrieval hunt quickly.

Burtevertree looked for the tree while Lorimorning drove the truck. The trees looked a lot alike, and they had checked out several likely-looking trees, also pausing for snacks, before they found the hiding place. There was still enough hydrogen in the airbag to offset the weight of the vehicle, so it was not hard for the two to get it into the back of the truck; then they quickly drove back to the truck's hiding place. Being spotted by a couple from the lakeside town, the responsibility for getting the experimental air vehicle out of the truck and back to the lakeside town was left up to them, and Burtevertree and Lorimorning wearily hiked over to the skiff that took them to the cave opening, and they hiked the kilometer-long cave tunnel, briefly rested in their small nook there at the cave entrance, then headed for their long term home out in the forest.

A couple days later, the lakeside town's educational museum specialists came to the forest home, requesting that Burtevertree participate in making a photograph of the experimental airship being used. Their scientists had invented a process where a surface being sandblasted by very fine-grained particulates, would shift from a random pattern to areas of more or less concentration, as varied by the pattern of heating effects of an intense light image that was focused on the surface being sandblasted. They needed Burtevertree to make another brief flight in the vehicle, just a few feet off the ground; it was to be a posed image with Lorimorning in the photo too, she in the process of handing him a package of food and drink.

Rather curious as to what this was all about, the next day, Burtevertree and Lorimorning hiked through their forest to the seedship site, surprised at how nice it looked, mounted aboveground as a permanent museum exhibit. There was a well-made path leading out into the forest from there; following it out, they found a clearing where several structures were in the process of being built; this was the new research station for the lakeside town's folks. Several projects were ongoing, and one of them was the image sandblasting apparatus. Some very smooth pieces of thin sandstone rock were there, and several had patterns engraved into them by the process as it was being developed. Images of the encampment and some of the experimenters were clearly visible on some of the rock surfaces, and some smaller ones were examples of an inked roller having gone across such an engraving, wetting only the raised areas, and producing a much clearer image. These all were going into an educational museum exhibit here, telling about the development of the process. For now, they were ready for the photograph to be made of the airship in use; Burtevertree got into the harness, this time in a more dignified manner with the hydrogen bag already inflated a bit more than needed just to lift the unloaded airship's weight, while it was actually tethered to the ground.

The energy storage wheels were not spun up for this photograph; the photo needed to show the airscrew and not be a blur. In fact, all had to be motionless for about a whole second while the photoengraving was being done, assisted by a sun angle just right. Lorimorning held up a package of snacks and a jug of water; Burtevertree reached down with one hand touching the objects; motionless a few seconds and were told it was done. The tethered airbag vehicle was lowered the few feet, Burtevertree unloosed himself, and the two enjoyed eating the munchies together while they watched the process of removing the sandblasted stone sheet. And yes, there they were, engraved into the stone, recognizably.

The floating airship was pulled along over to a partially built structure, taken inside and fairly permanently anchored there. The plate with the image showing it in use was fitted into a wall panel next to the crudely-built propelled airship; for now, it was to be held in place by its airbag filled with hydrogen enough to support the vehicle's weight along with some steel sections that approximated a person's weight, and were attached by the straps that originally held arms and legs.

30 ENERGY FROM THE HUMMING WIRE

The airship and photographic process educational museum facility was expected to be a major area of interest. Its location had been selected because it was the endpoint of a long cable group anchored there. One was a sliding cable, where a person up near the base of the Humming Wire tower, could either get into a harness, or even just hang on tight to a ring that would be carried on the belt of each worker up there, and in emergency the ring clamp could be quickly put around the sliding cable up there and the person would then rapidly slide down here. Currently it was an amusement ride, but it was also intended to be an escape route for people up at the facility being built up at the base of the Humming Wire tower; the now well-traveled path crossed the road and was at risk of leading Tealers to the facility. If there was a surprise raid by the Tealers, people could rapidly escape down the slide wire.

And in more peaceful times, the other pair of cables were actually a loop on a set of two pulleys, one set at the bottom here, and the other set up on the top of the cliff next to the tower base. They had two sets of apparatus on the cables, the one down here having a seat for a pair of riders, a small basket for carrying some objects, and another basket next to a variety of sizes of rocks. In use, a couple people with some carried items would get on and transfer rocks until a balance showed the sum weight had reached a standard overall weight. The same process was done at the same time at the top of the cliff, another pair of people getting on, or cargo equal to a person's weight along with half again cargo, then the balancing weight rocks; and when both top and bottom seating weighed the same, a fairly simple hand crank on the cable, pulled it around, swapping places of the top and bottom seating. Thus it was easy for a lakeside town couple to now get up or down between the two facilities.

It was considered fairly safe from Tealer invasion, since it took full cooperation between top and bottom to make the pulley lift work; and there was an emergency bar that could be rapidly swung into place that would whack an invading rider rapidly sliding down the slide cable, incapacitating them a lot, and hopefully then would be easily bound and secured by people down here. The keeper of the belt locking rings up at the top would always be on duty, ready to give rings out to lakeside folks up to the point of being overrun by invading Tealers, then him or herself escape down carrying any unused lock rings to prevent further use of the slide cable system.

Burtevertree and Lorimorning declined to experience the system right now, even though it looked interesting and a bit fun; they tended to already have more adventure than was comfortable for them, in their everyday life.

They did, however, ask why all this was being built, clearly it had to do with the facility being built on top of the cliff, at the base of the Humming Wire tower. They would have to go up to see, they were told; so up they went on the balanced cable pulley system, to the top of the cliff. Again, several structures were in the process of being built and put to use even while being built, up near the base of the Humming Wire tower. Part of the research and development being done there was to investigate the phenomenon they had noticed, that the area of the large metal screened area adjacent to the tower, would rapidly lose its snow in winter; and this was due to it being warmer there on the topside of the screen; and it was that way day and night. They wanted to know what provided the energy for all the heat.

They also had built a holding tank to store water that would melt off the screen area during the winter soon to arrive; it would be a supply of drinking and cleaning water for a year-around occupancy of the facility, they hoped. It was also known that the snow only melted on the upper part of the wire mesh screen, but did not melt much below the metal grid. Clearly it was some kind of energy light, like sunlight coming down from above onto the screen, but did not come down very far from the edge of the screen. So they were building residences and labs under the screen, to keep out the snow for work there during the winter, and the melt off their roofs would help fill the water holding tank. Some of the intended research was to explore the qualities of the invisible sunlight that came down to the top of the screen grid even in the night, and determine a direction if possible. Another area of research was to explore the obvious connection between this screen grid and the adjacent tower base for the Humming Wire; it seemed likely that it was a power source being used to somehow maintain the high velocity Humming Wire thing; all processes would have losses efficient or not, and would require a supply of energy to replace that which was lost in the system. This was a new kind of area for the lakeside town's science folks, and the engineering and manufacturing specialists were already in process of making new instruments for this research.

The first snow had fallen before the engineers had the craftspeople build a mockup of the shape of a section of the seedship's outer perimeter. They had found that a pull wire from the control area of the seed ship would open up the covering, and would expose the two energy storage rings that apparently stored energy for moving the seedship around. They guessed that the opening would exactly fit to the edge of the Humming Wire. So Burtevertree and Lorimorning were requested to use the tethered airship one more time before winter set in. Up they went, cranking on the various tethers until placing themselves just a meter from the edge of the Humming Wire. The scientists and engineers down below were envious of them, actually able to see the Humming Wire closer than anyone else had ever done, but they did not have the familiarity and skill in flying the tethered airship.

From a few feet away from the edge of the Humming wire, they could see that it was not a wire at all, but a ribbon. Actually it seemed like several ribbons, the ones on top going one direction very fast, and just under it was another set of ribbons going very fast in the opposite direction. Examining the mockup given them, and holding it a few inches from the edge of the Humming Wire ribbon, it looked like the Humming Wire, if magnetic, could inductively drag-transfer some energy to the edges of energy storage rings such as encircled the seed ship.

The mockup did not have the huge energy storage rings to inductively drag to higher speed, but it did have a set of electrical coils connected to small incandescent bulbs. Very carefully Burtevertree inched the mockup close to the edge of the Humming Wire, and yes, various incandescent lights began to glow, some dimly, others brightly. The instructions were to observe the lights while getting closer to the humming wire, getting no closer than two centimeters; but before that, several sets of small incandescent lamps had glowed so brightly that they had burned out. Holding the mockup at the required distance, for a moment, Lorimorning marked the symbols for intensities on the drawing they had been supplied; then carefully they eased away from the edge of the Humming Wire, getting a real sense that getting too close could cause a lot of damage.

Back down on the ground level, they handed the mockup and the drawing to the eager scientists, Lorimorning giving some verbal additions, pointing at the now blackened incandescent bulbs, knowing that the scientists were going to have to quantify the levels of inductive energy at distances from the Humming Wire, from this experiment's data. Yet they all knew already that it was very likely that this was where and how the seed ship got its energy put into its huge energy storage rings. It would have needed to fly up to the edge of the Humming Wire, open the access hatch and gently move the airship to contact the humming wire portal.

While up there at the humming wire, Lorimorning noticed that there was a large groove near the top of the tower, and the humming wire passed along the edge of the groove; she suggested that in practice, that would be where the seed ship would nudge its outer edge into that groove, which would both align the seed ship's energy rings to the humming wire, while also defining the relative distance between all the surfaces. The groove was not very apparent from the ground, among the other projections from the tower, but when Lorimorning pointed at them, the lakeside town's scientists saw what she was pointing at. The whole coupling method was becoming apparent and seemed reasonable. Burtevertree suggested that after the mockup was fully measured as to the effects of the fields, that it could have wires attached to one of the coils, and the mockup be temporarily fastened into the groove up at the humming wire pathway, and use the induced electricity that came down the wires, to provide a little energy to the research facility, which especially would be welcome in winter weather.

And a few days later, while it was beginning to snow consistently, the lakeside scientists begged that the tethered airship be used one more time, to do exactly what had been suggested. Up they went, Lorimorning moving them back into proximity of the groove linking the humming wire's edge, and they placed the modified mockup section there, lashing it to projections on the tower. As they hurriedly used the tethers to lower their airship down past the edge of the cliff, they were rewarded by seeing the bright glow of lights down at the base of the tower.

Dusk was falling and the snow was falling faster too, and by the time the airship had been secured for the winter, it was both too dark and the snow too deep to make a run for home with the children. There were three couples from the lakeside town's educational museum staff that were going to spend the winter there, and they loaned Lorimorning and Burtevertree and their two children some blankets; they went inside the seedship for cover, ate some cold food and snuggled down for the night.

31 SNOW TUNNEL WORLD

Morning's dim dawn showed that it was a severe snowstorm, several feet of snow had already accumulated and was still falling fast. They had to get to their winter home out in the forest, even for their next meal. Burtevertree used one of the shovels left there from the digging out of the seedship, to dig the snow off of a single lane path towards home; he dug until tired, then returned along his path. By the time he got back to the seed ship, another inch of snow was on the trail. So Lorimorning picked up a second shovel, and all four of them headed down the trail, and Lorimorning began to dig the path. Half an hour later, Burtevertree went in front and resumed the digging; they alternated that way, making sure neither got really tired before swapping front digging. They knew they were getting close to the cave entrance, recognizing the trail features; then they were going up the steps and into the front of the cave. They had minimal supplies stashed there, but the food and blankets were very welcome, resting there the remainder of the day and slept the night there.

The next morning showed the massive snowstorm characteristic of the season; the snow was already about five feet deep. If they managed to get back to the seed ship museum site, they might be able to get food shared by the folks there, but they were not likely to have much more stored there than they themselves needed to make it through the winter. So Burtevertree began the slow process of digging out a section of the trail towards the forest home, making it into a packed snow arch. It was slow work, but the arch kept the falling snow from filling in where the trail had been dug. Lorimorning observed how he was doing it, then insisted he take a break while she took over the task.

They resumed this early the next morning; they only had two more days of supplies remaining stashed there at the cave entrance. They had not included a lot of firewood, so they were having a warming fire lit only a couple of times each day. Burtevertree remembered his first winter making a snow tunnel, and he made the tunnel now right along the edge of the well-worn trail here, close enough to gather some of the edibles from the branches at the edge of the path, along with a bit of deadwood to add to their fire supplies.

They were all very weary and hungry by the time they had gotten to the doorway of their forest home. But soon they were getting warmed in there by a cook-fire, and a real hot meal was enjoyed by them all before taking a long rest.

Yet after a couple of days in their house, spending the time sealing up drafty areas in the wall that had not been adequately readied for winter, they were needing to go do something, anything. So they all set out, carrying shovels, and sacks of provisions, to re-stock the cave entrance stash with emergency supplies. This gave them opportunity to examine the condition of their new snow tunnel; it had collapsed in a couple of places near the cave entrance, but now was easier to make a stronger arch with the now deeper snow. The long pathway would be a way to get exercise through the winter, they decided, yet they also needed to be able to survive a major collapse of the snow tunnel even if they were out away from home. They decided to stay at home for a few more days, then repeat the inspection trip to the cave entrance.

Gaining confidence, they then rather casually began to dig out and pack an archway through the snow toward the site of the seedship facility. No hurry, but it gave them some exercise, and thought it could become useful, to be able to get over to the seed ship museum facilities during the long winter. It took over a week to extend the snow tunnel to the seedship, then they surprised the three lakeside town museum couples staff living on site there; they too had been finding it some struggle in the deep snow, and were eager to travel the snow tunnel that had been built. They had kept the dual cable pulley out of snow burial that connected them to the top of the cliff; but they were realizing that those people up there were no longer able to connect with the lakeside town itself, and instead of being a potential source of emergency supplies, were instead probably worrying about not having enough food for the winter.

Burtevertree pointed out that there was now a way to travel to the cave and then the tunnel would take them to the edge of the lake; perhaps from there they could get to the town. One of the couples from the humming-wire facilities volunteered to see if that would work, and coming down the pulley tramway, they then were shown through the snow tunnel to the cave entrance, then shown how to go through the cave tunnel and find the opening at the edge of the lake. The skiff tied up there was now frozen solid in the ice, but the ice was able to bear a person's weight, so the couple set off toward the town, walking across the ice while staying near the edge of the frozen lake, in case they broke through; plus they would be sure not to wander the wrong way in the heavy continuing snow storm. Lorimorning handed them a bag of food, wished them safe journey, reminded the couple to bring back not just food and other supplies, but bring one of their battery-assisted hand crank flashlights when they came back, so they could find their way through the cave tunnel, since there would be no one to meet them at the cave entrance, most likely.

The lakeside town couple vanished across the ice in the snowstorm, the snow already building up on top of the frozen lake's water; Burtevertree called out to the couple to also bring along a twine to show the way back to the cave tunnel; along which eventually they would need to make a snow tunnel for regular commutes during the next several months.

The lakeside town folks assured them that they were a bit

familiar with the lake in winter, but had never ventured out this far; wintertime was for staying indoors and building educational museum exhibits, as well as for concentrating on learning from the huge collection of educational museum exhibits that already taught all that they knew. Some things were taught through exhibits of book form, but the fully experienceable 3D material exhibits taught so much more about the nature of things and the ways of engineering and manufacturing craftsmanship.

However, soon Lorimorning was surprised to hear voices outside their forest home; opening the door, they found two of the lakeside town's educational specialists and a dozen children. The lakeside town's folk had teamed up together to learn this new snow tunneling process, had built a tunnel from the town across the lake to the cave tunnel, and this was a museum class trip over here to experience the extent of the snow tunnel system, and to visit the inventors of the technique to say thanks. With the snow tunnels, it was almost not like winter now, as they could travel so far without struggling in the deep snow and the cold that still existed but now was mostly outside their new passageways. Hundreds of the lakeside town couples had now taken the museum's snow tunnel construction training, which involved building onto the snow tunnel across the frozen lake, and with so many doing the work, it went fast and easily, the couples doing the construction for the fun of doing it as part of learning.

They were also in the process of building snow tunnels over to the stockade where the Tealers were held captive, and also to the shelter that housed the rescued non-Tealer bachelors from the Tealer's town, which would make it easier to bring provisions to both sets of men. Those who had the task of bringing food to those groups were already stressed from the struggle through the snow to take food over, but also just seeing so many men without coupled women, reminded them of that horrible way of life that the Tealer's created and enforced for their reproductive use. Yet it also reminded the lakeside town's folks that the Tealer's would eventually attempt to assault and take over their town; and yet also reminded them that they were just slightly-warped humans, not monsters.

The best part was noticing the subtle change in behavior of the captive Tealers, as they ate food that included some of the newly found grain that apparently supplied a missing protein that was related to the Tealer genetics, causing them to act like monsters if it was missing. Although they had grown up with no practice at being anything but ever combative and endlessly showing superiority to others, they at least now seemed to be a bit less instinctively assaultive in all that they did.

However, the captive Tealers seemed very stressed out without having a ball to be constantly bouncing back and forth amongst themselves; although it seemed part of their obnoxious social coordination and communication system; and therefore doing without a ball to use, stopped that behavior. But the lakeside towns folks had decided to bring a ball from their town, and gave it to the Tealers along with food one day. And soon the Tealers were much happier, bouncing the ball amongst themselves. Yet it was not a Tealer ball, and they seemed more thoughtful as time went on. Along with the small amount of the previously missing grain protein in their diet, and the ball bouncing of a non-Tealer-made ball, they had noticeably become more self-aware in their ball game playing obsession, as if a bit aware that they were playing the game as individuals instead of being one large organism composed of many Tealer men acting in total coordination.

And now with a snow tunnel to soon be completed to reach their compound, it would be easier to provision them. Several museum educator couples planned to routinely go study the Tealer men as if they were a museum exhibit, despite the ugly mode of life of a bunch of men without women as partners, having to be observed. That study task seemed a bit like latrine duty to the couples assigned to study the Tealers; but, such things needed to be done in the fulness of the world of knowledge.

32   WHAT CAUSED THE ENERGY DROP

Lorimorning thanked the group of educators for that information about the captive Tealers and expansion of the snow tunnel system by the Lakeside town's folks. She well remembered the extreme effort it had taken for she and Burtevertree to get the snow tunnel made from the seed ship site over to here. However, she expressed concern that now, if the Tealers were their usual deceptive characters with unexpected physical strength and coordination amongst themselves, that they might find a way to escape and might end up at Lorimorning and Burtevertree's door without warning.

Still, the little crowd of two couples and a dozen students were brought in a few at a time, and shown around in the forest home. Burtevertree realized that it must seem primitive, all built without the accumulation of knowledge and skills of the lakeside town-folk; but everyone was polite, only interested in what was done to build it all within the forest resource scenario.

They did ask how did they make a small steam engine driven electric generator and make a battery and lights with only these resources, however. Burtevertree then had to explain the wreckage of two of the Tealer's utility trucks and the survival of he and Lorimorning despite their injuries, unlike the hundreds of other human remains of non-celibate non-Tealer men that had been eliminated by the Tealers over the many decades. The steam engine was the main starter engine from one of the fallen trucks, and the generator and battery were from the truck too.

The lakeside folks pointed out that the other fallen truck might also have such a steam engine, could they have it? Burtevertree said it all was there for the taking; and if possible, please properly bury any human remains they found along the way while scrounging for parts from the wrecked trucks. He then drew a map of roughly where the cliff-bottom mess area was, saying it was up to the lakeside folks to make the tunnel over there this time, not his job anymore. Besides, it brought back too many unpleasant memories for he and Lorimorning, over there in the mess. The lakeside town couples assured them that the snow tunnel extension over to the messy site would be done by the townsfolk, working in relays of couples doing digging, compacting and laying up snow archway a half hour per couple. It would get built rapidly. And would it be alright if necessary, to come to get further advise?

When the museum class had left, vanishing down the snow tunnel and voices faded away, both Lorimorning and Burtevertree breathed a sigh of relief. Their snug little home had never been so packed with people, all of them inquisitive about everything. They even now looked at their home with a bit different awareness, due to the process.

Still, with all their food storage and preparation for this winter, they no longer were in constant survival struggle. They got bored, and so they traveled the snow tunnels over to the seed ship museum facilities. Leaving their children to be students being taught there, they rode up the pulley lift chair transport system up to the base of the humming-wire tower, with the excuse of bringing some bags of special food and supplies provided by the lakeside town folks.

Soon they were being shown around the housing and labs that were built up here, and were being supplied energy from the electrical pickup coil up near the top of the tower, placed there by Burtevertree and Lorimorning a month ago. Discussion amongst the lab folks there included speculation about what if there were still seedships out there, needing to come here to have their propulsion energy replenished by the humming wire; they would find that the access slot was already occupied by the mockup and pickup coil lashed into place there. And they also pointed out that the crashed seed ship was probably caused by not having quite enough energy remaining to make it to the spin-up location on top of the tower. And that had led to there being missing species in the biosystem, such as the grain that supplied an essential protein that was possibly the cause of the Tealer's coming into being and wreaking so much misery on others as a result. What if there were still more seed ships out there, and would need to come here to be replenished?

Others said that the seed ship had crashed about a hundred years ago, and probably the seeding of the planet had ceased long ago. And maybe there had never been but the one seed ship, now crashed. Yet the educational museum teams were not the type to simply compose in abstract. They had located wires that connected the strange power reception grid above them, over under the ground and into the base of the tower. They had found where the wires were attached; and had carefully attached their own wires to a similar junction on the wire mesh grid above them, and now it was being studied as being a more direct source of energy. It was over a hundred volts, far more than any of their equipment could utilize, however. Their batteries were 24 Volts, and the voltage from the wire mesh was about five times that voltage.

Burtevertree asked about their batteries on hand; there were ten batteries, available as backup energy sources. Burtevertree then suggested hooking up five of the batteries in series, and putting them all as a load to the overhead energy source, using an incandescent lamp bulb in series with the batteries, a small lamp and a high current lamp. Hooking it up, the small lamp made a bright flash of light and burned open. Bypassing it with a wire jumper, the high current lamp glowed a dull red; energy was flowing into the batteries. They then could see that any one of the batteries' connectors could be a useful energy source for their lights and equipment. Yet there would need to be an overall near equality of load across each battery on the average, since all would get the same charging current.

The engineers there quickly changed from the battery system to a series group of high current incandescent bulbs, all glowing a dull red; it produced very welcome heat; and across any bulb, they could parallel other smaller brighter bulbs and electronic instruments.

They were careful to verify that the voltage being delivered to the humming wire's tower was not dropped more than a fraction, protecting the facility's power usage. They did not want the humming wire to fail at whatever it was doing; surely it did more than provide an occasional power boost to a seed ship.

A week later found Burtevertree and Lorimorning again in the multi-tethered airship, despite the cold and heavy snow ongoing. They floated up to near the slot next to the humming wire, and removed the mockup with its power pickup from the slot, freeing it for possible use by other seedships. While up there, they also made a quick clay impression of the other projections and slots at the top of the tower, then brought it all down to the waiting scientists, now freed of responsibility for possible seedship crashes, and now having the clay mold for making a model of the top of the tower with its odd structures, something to help guess further purposes of the humming wire and its tower. The airship was then again secured for the winter, and they returned home with their children, the double dose of adventure was enough to satisfy them for awhile. The prepared winter comforts of their expanded forest home was much appreciated, as they relaxed into the winter shut-in lifestyle.

The peacefulness did not last long, however. One morning the sound of a noise was perceptible, then slowly gaining in loudness; it sounded a bit like the humming wire, but enormously louder. Still increasing in loudness a couple of hours later, Burtevertree bored a side hole into his snow tunnel a ways from the doorway to their home, and poked his head up into the swirling snowfall. The snow was already much deeper than he had seen it before, too. Turning his head around, it seemed that the sound was most intense off in the opposite direction to the humming wire tower; the humming wire was horizontal and stretched across their sunken canyon, and the wire had vanished into the distance toward the other side of the canyon. They had wondered if there were another tower there too; maybe the thing went clear around the planet.

Listening to the increasing sound off in the direction of the other side of the canyon, the sound reduced in volume then suddenly ceased. All was quiet again. He pulled down into the tunnel, plugged the hole up to keep the cold air out, returned inside their home. What was that all about?

They packed up survival gear; the winter could become very hazardous out there, they knew, if things went wrong, a tunnel collapse, whatever. An hour later they were at the facilities at the base of the humming wire tower, half their survival gear left with the children at the museum facilities at the seedship. They arrived just in time to find everybody engrossed in making measurements of everything they could measure, and the sound was getting louder again, and clearly was the humming wire. The tower itself was too strong to transmit the vibration, but from far across the valley, came the sound, and now it seemed to be again getting louder. A couple who were outside measuring effects on the snow, suddenly burst inside to say that something had slid along the humming wire toward them. The vibrations stopped; everybody went outside, warmly clothed or not, and stared up into the falling snowstorm towards the top of the tower. The humming sound now seemed only a little louder than it had always sounded before.

There seemed to be a large dark object up there, sitting on the humming wire, yet also anchored to the top of the tower. They heard a voice call out; it sounded a bit like a greeting but the expression not quite standard language. "Hello, hello" again called out the voice. A hinged wire ladder dropped down from the object up there, and soon the figure of a person came down the ladder. Clothed in some kind of thin insulation, up close, it was clearly a woman. Lorimorning went out to cautiously say "hello" back to the stranger; and soon despite the peculiarities between their talk, another figure came down the ladder, a man this time, and that couple went inside the facilities of the lakeside folks scientists. The small drop in energy here at this tower had been observed at headquarters, and the couple had been sent to find out what was causing the power drop. It was much better to find that people were causing it, instead of some major natural phenomena; the snowstorm's effect on the power beam and humming wire was well known, and the variation from the norm had to be checked out.

33   HEADQUARTERS DECISION

The newcomers were impressed with the science facilities here, and the primitive but efficient means for availing themselves of the new-found power source. However, it was requested that there be no more than ten percent more energy drawn from the system by the lakeside town's facilities. During summer they could take another 5% energy. But for now please don't use much more energy; it was needed to maintain the high velocity centrifugal support of the carousel which the lakeside towns folk called the humming-wire.

One thing could be done to supply more energy to the lakeside town's facilities, is to create another energy beam like that which served the power rectenna here at this tower. To enable a bit more security for the facility, they would beam it down into a site in the canyon below, in the center of the sunken canyon. To prepare for it, the lakeside town's engineering and manufacturing needed to make a wire grid with rectifiers connecting between them, and output wiring to deliver the resulting input energy to their facilities. It would take about a month to get the energy beam set up for there, and that ought to give the lakeside people time to build at least a small part of a sample section of a wire grid, which could be carried around measuring voltage generated across it, to determine the exact location area of the new energy beam.

The lakeside town scientists asked what was a rectifying diode. As if shocked, the newcomers finally commented to themselves that the knowledge repository to be delivered to this planet must have not gotten here, or was delivered wrongly. The implications about the knowledge state of these people down here was beginning to sink in to their consciousness. Asking about semiconductor signal conditioners, they got more blank looks.

Yet it was apparent that the lakeside town's folks had made fine advances in engineering, and their educational system must be comparably functional. How did it work? They decided to stay here a bit longer, researching the educational processes being utilized.

Yes, there was another tower on the far rim of the canyon here, and that is where this small shuttle is usually parked, for use to come over here to service this accelerator. Did the people not know that?

The crash of the seed ship soon provided explanation of a lot of things. For one thing, the knowledge banks had not been able to make it to the people being seeded here, obviously. The new couple then paused, grasping the implications of the culture here, surviving on minimal knowledge and missing significant amounts of biodiversity to support them. When learning about the menace of the Tealers, the newcomers seemed very distressed; it was thought that one of the grains would suppress those genes in the people who had them; those people had caused enormous harm to people and the environment of the home planet, and did not dare to be loosed here in this new world being seeded.

But what to do about the Tealers was not obvious. They were like a huge vicious wild animal gone berserk destroying everything it could in its obsession to eliminate all male genes other than its own aggressive genes. That the grain had just recently been discovered in the seed ship's wreckage and had already been found to provide needed nutrition for everybody, and also had a calming effect on the captive Tealers, indicated that it was the correct nutrition that originally was to have prevented the Tealer type behavior from coming into existence. This was terrible news; so much work had gone into bringing life to this formerly lifeless planet, and now it was at risk of being taken over by horribly broken men. Even this transportation system was at risk if the Tealer's found it; it was well known that the special management skills of the correctly functioning Tealer genes helped coordinate big projects; but if run-amok like now, they might destroy the humming wire or worse take it over and spread like a disease beyond the planet.

That was not tolerated; if the Tealers could not be brought into harmony with the rest of the living system on the planet, the transportation structure would have to be destroyed, and the planet quarantined from contact with the rest of mankind. It had happened once before, and that planet was abandoned to a terrible existence with most of the people enslaved by the Tealer type, and the planet's resources ravaged just for the Tealer's insatiable urges for power over other people and associated wealth.

As the newcomer couple turned to leave, they said they would return in two years, to verify that the people here had terminated the Tealer behavior menace; if it had not been accomplished, this humming-wire would be destroyed, and the planet declared infested, and all would have to endure the abuse of the Tealers from then on. If there was any attempt by the Tealers to take over this facility here, it would be destroyed; the Tealers must not be allowed to spread. They were sorry they could not help restrain the Tealers, but there was hope since the needed grain was now in the lakeside town's hands. But the Tealer type historically would not allow the nutrition to be given to them, and they were supremely capable of preventing anything they chose to prevent.

Burtevertree got in one more question, asking what was the humming-wire and its towers. Sure, was the answer, it is the usual planetary access system for sustained colonization efforts. These two towers were powered by satellites in orbit high overhead, energy from the sun day and night, beamed down to the wire grid nearby. The humming wires were actually ribbons, and one set of ribbons encircled the planet at about this same altitude, there being three more such towers in that circle around the planet; the other set of ribbons went much faster and their much higher centrifugal force stretched them out to reach synchronous orbit high above the farside of the planet. That was where headquarters is located. If the people here needed to communicate with headquarters, there was a communications station at the base of the tower; going over to the base of the tower, he pulled a lever and a panel swung open. Another lever activated a vision screen and audio link; he said into it that the comm link was being demonstrated to the planetary seed-folk here.

There was much that was hoped to be learned from this establishment of life on this planet. One of them clearly was the paperless educational system, the vast collection of museum interactive exhibits that taught everything from language beginnings to engineering ways. Surely this needs to be further developed and eventually made available to the larger interplanetary civilization. It was a fine adaptation to the loss of the knowledge base that had somehow gotten lost here, due to the crash of the seed ship; the automated system had apparently delivered both copies of the knowledge base to the living system that was set up on the continent on the other side of this planet.

But that they were struggling with a Tealer-infestation of humanity, and might not be able to stop the infestation, was a dire situation. It was estimated they would have two years to remove the infestation or be absorbed by it, per historical records of this kind of situation. The newcomers then climbed up the wire link ladder; it vanished up into the snowstorm, and the humming got a bit louder as the dark object slid out along the humming wire out across the canyon, leaving everybody silent and alone with the Tealer problem, now realizing that it was a worse situation than they realized.

Yet they had the needed nutritional grain. Burtevertree suggested that somehow the Tealers not be able to obtain any food which did not contain enough of the new grain, and arrange it to be totally that way by the second crop, and the first crop have at least some of the new grain mixed in with everybody's food. It would then be a race between nutrition's normalizing effect versus the wild craving for power and control, wanting to stay in power and control with total obsession that was the Tealer epigenetics without the required nutrition from the grain, and would eventually realize that obsession was fading away if they consumed the added nutrition. The fate of their world depended on this nutritional technique; would their children be evermore ruled by power maniacs, or would the Tealer genes be brought back into its normal helpful harmonious functioning as part of human genes.

They looked up into the falling snow, hearing a louder rumble from far across the canyon as the captive spaceship rode the humming wire carousel up the eccentric hoop to orbit far above the other side of the planet, they now knew. There was a much larger reality to existence. Yet their misfortune that had activated the Tealer epigenetics could doom their world to isolation from the larger civilization of planets, due to the need to quarantine this planet due to the infestation of the Tealer genetics run amok as it had done so on other planets in the past; no one wanted the Tealer kind to be loose amongst their peoples. Better that this planet be isolated and left to destroy itself; they knew the end result of when the Tealer genes went totally dominant.

But it was not the way of civilization to act to destroy all life on this planet, back to the way it was before; that would be a Tealer way. However, the peoples and whole ecosystem would have to suffer under the rule of the Tealers until eventually the Tealers would destroy the entire ecosystem and then all perish from lack of that which enabled their life. It had happened on other planets; the recording of it had made many soap opera series, but now no longer was anything less than boring and disgusting.

Still, this planet seemed to have a chance to get their overall human genes back into balance, and be able to build a long lasting civilization and a dynamic balanced ecosystem as part of it.

Wearily the record of this planet was closed up in headquarters high above the planet in geostationary planetary orbit. Technology was not perfect and in this case had enabled a seed ship to not make it back to be reenergized by the carousel hoop, the humming-wire, as the colonists called it; and it had caused the loss of both the essential nutrition to prevent expression of the Tealer genes, and of loss of the initial colonization knowledge resource set.

That the colonists had done so well, was useful data; perhaps their self-sufficient ingenuity that had created the museum educational system, and had also identified the Tealer gene males and had expelled them, would find ways to subdue and normalize the expression of the Tealer genetic males bent on making the planet populated only by Tealer males through treachery and violence; clearing all that away somehow and then all could become normalized and thriving as originally intended for this planet.

The record sealed for the next two years; then headquarters was vacated. What kind of stew would ultimately result on the unfortunate planet below, was not their concern anymore.

ABOUT THE AUTHOR

Changing over from futilely attempting to get supportive help from reaction-engine based aerospace corporations and NASA, such as for building hoop-type electrically powered centrifugally self-supported ground to high earth orbit transportation systems, by writing formal technical papers and presenting them at technical space conferences, Jim Cline at first resented the need to describe his technical concepts as if mere science fiction. But once into the spirit of writing sci fi high tech adventures, he found that mode of communicating his huge variety of space concepts and associated enabled space facilities via them being a framework on which to write sci fi adventure novels, he found that was a far more enjoyable way of life, instead of attempting to make rocket enthusiast corporations become railroad builders instead of glamorous rocket builders and users largely based on R&D already proven out by NASA at taxpayer expense, by communicating peer reviewed technical papers through suit, tie and PowerPoint presentation conference tasks. Writing high tech science fiction adventures, where at last his concepts can play out in the complex world, even if only in the imagination, is better than nothing; and through books it can even be shared. Jim has eight prior sci fi novels published in paperback and some as ebooks, all done as a hobby. See the list below. Enjoy!

Other Publications by James E. D. "Jim" Cline

Eight High-Tech Science Fiction Paperbacks:
Building Up
The Ark of 1984's Future

183

It's Down to Earth
The Torus Cities Ice Shields Returning Home
Going Past The Town Prison
Three Species On Lava World
Planetfall Twenty-Seven

Non-Fiction Formally Published Technical Papers:

Cline, J. E. David, "Treehouse Haven", Meditation Magazine, Winter 1990, 28-31

Cline, J. E. David "Wet Launch of Prefab Habitat Modules" Space Manufacturing 10, Pathways to the High Frontier, Space Studies Institute, AIAA, 1995, 88-91.

Cline, James E. D. "Kinetically Strengthened Transportation Structures" Space 2000 Conference Proceedings, American Society of Civil Engineers, 2000, 396-402.

Cline, James E. D. "Kinetically Supported Bridge Vehicle Lift To GEO" Space 2002 Robotics 2002 Conference Proceedings, ASCE, 2002, 8-21.

Cline, James E. D. "Energy Flow in Kinetically Strengthened Transportation Structure Systems to Space" Earth & Space 2004 Conference Proceedings, ASCE, 2004, 859-866.

Cline, James E. D. "The Space Escalator Carousel's Unique Potentials" Space Exploration 2005 Conference Proceedings, SESI, 2005, 230-238

Cline, James E. D. "Characteristics of Space Escalator Carousels vs. Space Elevators" Space Exploration 2005 Conference Proceedings, SESI, 2005, 355-364

Author's U-Tube channel: http://www.youtube.com/user/jedcline
Example: http://www.youtube.com/watch?v=V6fZQ_EULZw

Also see the author's website and blogs:
www.kestsgeo.com
email: jedcline2@kestsgeo.com
http://www.kestsgeojedc.blogspot.com
http://jedcline.wordpress.com